Stefan's Project

By: Ronald Wynn

Stefan's Project

Stefan's Project

By: Ronald Wynn

Ronald Wynn Productions, LLC

Ronald Wynn Productions, LLC

Copyright © 2014 Ronald Wynn

ISBN-10:   0-9755284-6-7

ISBN-13:   978-0-9755284-6-4

www.facebook.com/pages/penofpoet/133124886763140

www. Penofpoet. com

Cover Design: Ronald Wynn

Editor: Angie Collins Hewitson

Editor: Miriam Rowan

Manufactured in the United States of America

Dedicated to all those that believe in Love.

Stefan's Project

By: Ronald Wynn

A Bad Dream

The night nurses kept vigil over Stefan. They were attentive to him, the older ones felt motherly towards him. Often while sitting by his bedside they would hold his hand and silently weep. Sometimes he would curl up against them. Stefan's pillow was stained by his tears, it was heart breaking, the nurses often cried with him. The loss of love is tragic, but to see the person you love fall to their death is heart wrenching. In private, the nurses talked about the story and marveled over the romance. How incredibly sad; this young man whom clearly had reached a level of success every young man hoped to accomplish in their lifetime, lost the love of his life. How does something so tragic happen? They reminisced about what a movie the story would make and what a great novel it would be to read.

Julie the head nurse, said,
"He's such a handsome and talented young man this is so sad."

Stefan's story made them all think of their own husbands or boyfriends. Life is too short... Every moment is precious when you realize there is a chance it could be gone in an instant. What would you do if tomorrow were your last day? This story had everything Hollywood wanted – it would draw in the crowds. Yet, to Stefan it was not a movie; it was a nightmare, and he was the leading actor. The tragedy was real; there was no going home at the end of the day. There was no happy ending in sight. He was not interested in his story. He did not even want to know this story. Unfortunately, the story was his life. It was his tragedy. It was his eternal heartache, and it was killing him. He felt like he was dying inside.

He laid in his hospital bed in silence. He only spoke to ask for Amanda. The love of his life. He ignored the doctors when they asked if he was in pain.

Stefan would look at them with tears in his eyes. He wanted to scream at them about the pain. Unbearable, gut wrenching, heart stopping pain. The kind of pain that can not be stopped by medication. It was extremely hard to decipher emotional trauma from physical pain. Psychologists say a broken heart is more painful than a broken rib. There is no way to tell the difference while looking at a person who is crying. Stefan's cracked his rib, yet he could have cracked all of his ribs and not cared as long as Amanda was alive, but she was not. Stefan sat there staring at the light above his head. His thoughts were on Amanda.

A Mom to Hold

He heard a familiar voice in the doorway say,

"My boy. My boy."

Stefan's eyes filled with tears. The only person in the world to call him "boy" at twenty-seven years old was his mother. He slowly turned his head in the direction of the voice. The silhouette of a petite woman who had lived a tough life stood in the doorway. She endured many trials and tribulations, but this was a pain no mother is ever prepared for. For Stefan, his mother walking into the room was like God whispering, "It's okay now—everything will be okay." Stefan broke down and started crying. His mother came over to him, wrapped her arms around him, and held him tight. The nurse came to the doorway and watched as a mother held her child, a grown man who was still her little boy. The nurse had to wipe the tears from her eyes as Stefan continued to sob. It seemed like an hour that his mother just held him, telling him it would be okay.

"We don't always know why things happen in life."

Regardless, she was thankful to God that her boy was safe.

"I loved her, Mom. For the first time in my life, I loved someone, and... God took her away."

How does a mom respond to that?

"Hush, baby. God didn't take her away. It was her time. If anything, he let her spend that last week with you to see how wonderful Heaven would feel."

Again, Stefan said, "No, Mom. No!"
He started crying again.

"Stefan, I'm here to take you home. You're going to come home with me and stay with us for a little while. I need to spend time with my baby."

Stefan looked at her as she placed her hands on each side of his face and gently kissed his forehead. Stefan knew if he was ever going to get well, the only person who could help him was indeed his mom.

As they prepared to leave, Stefan's mom handed him a simple pair of jogging pants and t-shirt, along with an old, comfortable pair of his tennis shoes. wisely she put his hiking clothes   in a bag... Knowing that seeing the outfit he wore that night might upset him, she had brought him another change of clothes. Each of the nurses came in one by one and hugged Stefan.   Their embraces were deep and personal. He held onto each woman as if he were holding Amanda—and each nurse felt regretful, sorrowful, and filled with compassion and empathy. Stefan did not say anything. He just looked at them. It was as if he could not feel anything at that moment except sorrow and pain, he could barely breathe.

The doctor came into the room after talking with Julie in the hall way. He took a deep breath and then went over to Stefan.

"Stefan, I apologize; I did not tell the nurses that I need them to run some blood work to make sure everything is okay before you leave."

"Mrs. Rogers, if you don't mind could you come with me to my office. We seem to be missing some medical background information. Stefan… we will not be gone long."

Stefan's mother followed the doctor down the hall, past the nurses' station. She noticed that they were all wiping their eyes, looking at her and sniffling. The doctor closed the door. She knew something serious had happened.

"Mrs. Rogers… They found Amanda's body this morning."

They were both silent; the news was not surprising but, it was still painful to hear. Stefan's mom sat down; she could not speak. Her eyes filled with tears… she knew that this young woman was going to be her daughter-in-law, and this news confirmed Stefan's biggest fear. Hope was gone, how in the world was he going to be able to deal with this terrible news.

The doctor walked over and put his hand on her shoulder.

"We were all praying for a miracle. It is terrible news, plain terrible. Stefan does not know; I am not sure he is stable enough to hear it at the moment. I will come to your house when the time is right; you need to keep him away from the media. Mrs. Rogers, he may look fine on the outside. However, on the inside he is in bad shape. My concern is that even the funeral for Amanda might be too much for him to handle. I know it sounds awful not to tell him, but I have never seen a man more in love than Stefan is with that girl. As his doctor, I think it would put him in danger to attend. I am so sorry. The confirmation of her death could put him over the edge, causing him to shut down mentally."

Stefan's mom had trouble speaking; her voice shaking, she said,
"What do I do? I can't keep that from him." Clearly, she was upset at the news.
"My son loved her more than anything. He loved her."

There was a long pause as Mrs. Rogers looked out the window as though she was afraid to show how much she was hurting for her son inside. She turned to the doctor and said,
"Thank you for all you have done. We will call you when the time is right."

The doctor held her hand,

"Give it a little time, let him get home and be with family for a few days. Give me a call when you are ready, I will help you talk to him about it."

The doctor hugged Stefan's mom, two adults talking about the death of a young woman, a special woman.

Mrs. Rogers walked down the hall towards Stefan's room. She could see it in the eyes of the nurses that they had already heard the news. She wiped her eyes and stood in the doorway.

"We better get going, I told your father we would be home by noon."

Stefan stood up and gave Julie a hug. Her eyes filled with tears. She had trouble speaking, her heart was hurting because she knew how much Stefan loved Amanda. Stefan's mom spoke up,

"I am sure that Julie and the other nurses are going to miss you. Julie, we will send you a letter when we get home, your nursing staff has been so kind to Stefan. Thank you so much, I know you understand the difficulty of the situation."

Stefan's mom was telling the nurse to pull it together as much as she was telling her goodbye. She knew that Stefan was a smart guy, and if he realized the tears were about Amanda's death he would shut down, possibly for good.

"Julie do you mind going out to the car and opening the door?

Make sure that the radio is off, please. I have a terrible headache, right now music or talk radio is the last thing I need on the drive home. Oh—I almost forgot, could you call his father and tell him the news, so he knows we are running a little behind and will be home soon."

Julie understood she was making sure Stefan would not find out about Amanda on the radio. Julie also picked up on the fact that Mrs. Rogers wanted her to call his father and warn him about television and radio. Stefan held his mother's hand; they went out the front door of the hospital and got into her car. The nurses stood there watching him go, their hearts aching and their eyes filled with tears. A recovered body is never easy news, but in this case, it was clear that everyone had been hoping for a miracle.

Julie was the first to speak up.
"God, Amanda was a lucky girl to have him as a boyfriend. Intelligent, fit, sweet, honest and handsome, everything my husband is not!"

SkyVac 4

The helicopter transport alarm went off at the nurses station. This meant that an inbound helicopter was requesting permission to land.

"Saint Anthony, this is SkyVac 4, do you copy?"

SkyVac was a private search and rescue group used in dangerous extractions from canyons, forests, rivers—anywhere that others could not, or would not go. They boasted a reputation of the best in the country in search and rescue. Highly skilled and highly paid, the state contracted them in extreme cases or high profile accidents that required rescue or recovery.

Julie ran over and picked up the phone.

"SkyVac 4 this is Saint Anthony, we read you. Go ahead."

"Saint Anthony, this is SkyVac 4, we are inbound with a fall victim. We need an ER prep, portable lung, and head trauma specialist when we land. This one is hot; victim is unconscious, compound right tibia and femur, head trauma, possible spinal injury and collapsed lung; vitals are weak and unstable. Victim has been strapped on a lock board and mast (PSAG) has been installed.

ETA three minutes... over."

"SkyVac 4 you are clear for South platform, we will have a team ready for your arrival... over."

"Saint Anthony, this is SkyVac 4, switch to private please... over."

Julie switched the system to private mode; this enabled her to talk directly with the helicopter pilot without having to use air talk.

"SkyVac 4, this is Head Nurse Julie Dunaway, how can I help you?"

"Julie, this is Jim Patterson, the victim is Amanda Wilson, I repeat, we are inbound with Amanda Wilson... we are requesting a media lock out..."

Julie was stunned, "Jim, we were just told she had been recovered... not rescued."

"I know. This is a media blackout per the governor. We are 2 minutes out."

Julie's heart dropped; it was Amanda. The media was wrong or something. Whatever the case, it was irrelevant; because from the sounds of it she was in truly terrible shape. The term "HOT" meant that the patient had serious life threatening that could not be addressed in the helicopter. Injuries that were so severe that the patient might survive the three minutes to the landing pad.   Julie started getting her team together. Julie announced,

"All Class 'C' personnel only, everyone else please report to the North ER."

Julie's heart was pounding. Class 'C' were security cleared personnel only.

"Let's move it people—this is a 'hot' one, it is not a drill—this is the real thing. Page Doctors Sims and Hodgins."

Three minutes later the elevator doors from the roof flung open.

"Let's go, let's go people—move—time is something we do not have for this one."

Everyone was in place; Saint Anthony's Hospital was the best in the country for head trauma. Amanda was in the hands of the two best brain doctors in the country. Maybe it was luck, or maybe God arranged for the two doctors to be there for a one-day lecture. Either way it was a miracle she was even still alive

Going Home

As they were pulling out of the entrance of the hospital, Stefan's mom noticed a red and orange helicopter landing on the roof. She thought to herself how lucky she was that her son was alive. Her mind could not wander far; Stefan needed her attention.

Stefan was silent on the ride to his parents' home. Drowsy from the pain medication, he dozed off and on. When he was awake, Stefan stared out the window of the car, lost in his own thoughts. When he was awake he just sat there silently and watched the trees go by. His mother tried to engage him in conversation by telling him what had been going on with the family. Stefan had been too busy in his career to visit much with the family. He kept tabs on a lot of the family through social media,   the occasional email. However, it was not like the old days when the family was a big,   a massive unit where everyone knew what was going on and communicated with one another. As time progressed, parents grew older; and technology became more advanced. The younger generation stayed in touch, but the older generation seemed to fade away. Until, he only saw them in the background of photographs at birthday parties or other special events.

"Ted Morris passed away last week, he must have been in his late nineties."

Stefan turned his head and looked at her. It was just an

acknowledgement of what she was saying. Though Mr. Morris was a close friend of the family, Stefan had no room in his heart to care. He leaned his head back against the glass and looked out.

"Your father has been worried. He calls me every day asking how you are. He is terribly anxious to see you."

Again, Stefan lifted his head, instead of looking out the window he looked down at his hands and wrung them together. Maybe it was stress. Maybe it was an attempt to feel his feelings, but right then all Stefan thought about was Amanda and being alone.

Over the years, nothing changed except things got older and faded in color. Windows cracked and boards fell that used to hang straight. The old house still stood strong. It looked the same way it did the day he left. A small country home surrounded by hay fields in all directions. The cows looked the same; all black and white. It was like a snapshot of his youth, but very much in the present. Who says you can't go home, he thought.

Stefan walked around back and sat in his favorite swing.
"I will go and tell your father you're here. Do you want some lemonade?" His mom asked, as though he had just come home from school.
She was always taking care of him. Even when he went off to

college, she would constantly send him boxes of socks and shirts, new sheets for his bed, and even towels. It was so bad one year that he had to call her and say,

"Stop sending them. I have no room to put them. I still haven't even opened the ones you sent last time."

She still sent him packages but instead of random, she would label them.. Incase you don't make it home for your birthday etc... A reason to send her love. Stefan understood her need to mother him and he was grateful for the support.

A Child Once More

She brought him the lemonade as his father came to the back door and stood. Even at seventy years old, he still was not a man with whom you would want to pick a fight. Muscular, taller than average, but with a chiseled face that had seen so many bad things in life. He spent three years in a POW camp in Vietnam, a time in his life that no one talks about...he prefers it that way. It was private, and few people knew about it.

Mr. Rogers grew up on a farm. He was strong, handsome and was not afraid of anything. The war changed almost everything about him. He does not talk much, his muscles are mostly gone, and he is afraid of the darkness. Smiles are now few; after five years of Vietnam, he changed. Stefan's mom used to say that he always laughed and told jokes before he left for boot camp. The letters sent home were many. Initially, they were filled with hope, and a longing to come home. And then he stopped writing; Stefan's mom did not know if he was alive or dead. One Sunday after church, the Army Chaplain came to her house. She started crying before he even knocked on the door. He sat with her and her parents and told them the North Vietnamese had captured her husband—he was a prisoner of war. By the grace of God, he came home after three years in a POW camp; however, he came home a different man. He would wake up in the middle of the night saying the names of those lost. The dreams were so bad he slept with the light on. After the war, the smile went away, and the laughter never came back. Yet, he was a man of honor, and he loved his son.

His father stood in the doorway—probably because he was afraid that Stefan would see his tears. He stood there and waved.

"Glad to see you home, son. I'm sorry to hear what happened."

Stefan looked in his direction, gave a small wave, and went back to rocking back and forth in his swing. His mom brought over the lemonade. Stefan took a small drink, which was a big deal because he had not drunk much at the hospital. He had been on IV's, so it was not as if he was in danger of becoming dehydrated or malnourished. He just did not want to drink or eat anything. Quite frankly, he did not want to live.

His mom leaned over and kissed him on the forehead. "You come inside when you feel up to it, okay? I love you."

She walked back in the house feeling that everything was going to be okay. Stefan was going to pull through, but for a mother to see her child so devastated was very hard. She sat down on the old dog-patterned couch, put her hands on her face and started crying. How was she going to tell Stefan that Amanda's body had been found, Amanda had died?

"God, it's just not fair. Why? He's such a good kid. Why?"

Searching For Hope

Doctor Sims asked Jim from SkyVac and Julie to go over what had happened.
As the door closed, Julie spoke up first.

"What the hell is going on? The media reported Amanda's body had been recovered. If she is still alive, why would it be reported that way?"

Jim responded, "Julie, we were called two days ago because the local search parties had no experience in rock face searches. The governor called the office and told us it was an *'executive,'* search."

An *'executive,'* search means, no communication with the media, and SkyVac's was not to stop searching until they recover a body.

"Amanda has an 8-year-old brother named Michael, who is autistic. The parents did all they could to keep him away from the television and media, but unfortunately, he heard the news that Amanda was likely dead; there was little hope of finding her alive. He is having a terrible time with the news of her death. The media has been relentless in broadcasting all of the reasons they believed she was dead. The boy is not sleeping and cries constantly. He keeps telling his parents, 'Manda coming, Manda coming... supposed to be.' The family was desperate for answers, so they called the governor who was a personal friend of theirs. He then called us to help with the search; honestly, I did not have much faith in finding her alive... Amanda is a fighter."

"Why did not the media not pick this up?" Julie asked.

"After we explained her critical condition to her mom and Dad, they asked us not to go public for Michael's sake. Within minutes, we received a call from the governor. He had spoken with Amanda's parents; he asked us to leak only that we recovered a body. The media, as we expected, would assume she was dead and go public. You see, the family and the governor were aware that the chances of Amanda surviving her injuries were slim. They felt it was better to protect her brother than to cause worry about a truth that might only bring moments of happiness."

Doctor Sims responded,
"That's a big risk for him politically... the media likes crucifying good people. Jim... tell me more about the fall, the body position when you found her. Any indication that she was conscious at any point after the fall?"

"She was found at 26 feet below the face, she must have hit a ledge below which changed her descent, casting her body to the right. The thick tree growth she passed through made her difficult to find. We found one broken tree limb... that was it. We sent climbers over the edge to search; even they had trouble. Our team never questions a lead, we always follow it. She was through the brush and wedged upright between two rocks." Jim reached into his pocket and pulled out the camera that records body positions, last rights and other details that might be useful for legal issues or diagnoses. "Here are the images taken by our extract team."

"Unbelievable… My God—how in the world did she survive that?" Julie whispered.

"Julie, she has not survived this yet, this girl's got a fight on her hands."

Just then Doctor Hodgins came to the door,
"Doctor Sims, Do you have a minute to go over the scans? We have some pretty serious issues that need addressed as soon as possible."
The images of Amanda's body started appearing on multiple monitors. Jim was impressed. It was top of the line high definition equipment. Four 42-inch screens side by side gave doctors the ability to look at all angles of a scan. There were five 36-inch screens that showed live vital signs, brain activity and test results. Everything a doctor needed to make proper decisions before the doctor ever touched a knife was right there. Amanda's body was trying to speak in pictures; it was up to the doctors to find out what it was saying. There were several dark masses next to her right lung, which looked like an old deformed balloon half full of air. The break in the right

tibia would need a rod to hold it in place.

"Look at the right side of the hip bone; I have never seen one with that much damage in a patient still alive. The two rocks must have protected her from being torn up on the inside from broken bones." Doctor Hodgins said with a puzzled voice.

A nurse came to the door "Excuse me doctors, but she is still losing blood."
The doctors agreed they had no time to waste; they were going to have to do exploratory surgery—and soon.

Doctor Sims spoke in the same tone as his lectures,
"We will start at the hip, Julie can you page Doctor Wright down here? We need to set the broken bones as soon as possible, but if we cannot find out where she is bleeding, that's not going to matter is it?"

Both doctors went to scrub in, Jim headed back to the Helicopter. "Julie, please give me a call with an update as soon as you can."

"Will do Jim, thank you for what you guys do, you have given her a chance."

Doctor Sims and Hodgins worked on Amanda into the night. Nine hours might not seem like much; however, neither doctor had any sleep. They had both arrived early the morning before for the lecture.

As Doctor Hodgins pulled off the blood soaked gloves, he said. "That's it; we have done everything a man can do. It is up to Amanda and God."

Doctor Hodgins and Doctor Sims washed up and change into clean scrubs before heading to the O.R. waiting room to discuss the results of the surgery with Amanda's parents. Julie was with them as they walked in.

"Mr. and Mrs. Wilson, I am Doctor Hodgins, and this is Doctor Sims. We want you to know that your daughter is fighting hard. There has been a tremendous amount of blood loss. We had to induce a coma due to the severity of the head trauma and the swelling of the brain. The next 72 hours are going to be critical. Julie will take you in to see her, but I want you to know she will not look like your daughter. Talk to her; let her know you are here. We have found that many times people remember voices. We are not out of danger, far from it. Mrs. Wilson, Doctor Sims and I need to be honest with you. There is a strong chance she will not make it. If she does... well, we have no idea what is going on in her head or how much damage has occurred yet. Keep praying. I am staying in town for the next few days to make sure she gets the best care. Doctor Sims has to get back to New York for a few days and will return on Friday. I am so sorry you are facing this, but Amanda is in the best hands possible. She clearly is a fighter and my hopes and prayers are that we make it through the next 72 hours. Then the real battle begins..."

Doctors are never good at sweet talk. In fact, they tend to tell the truth even if it causes the heart to ache. Both doctors have watched many times as mothers collapsed and fathers went into cardiac arrest when they heard the news about their child's condition. Both men were fathers, so dealing with children... even adult children was always difficult. Doctor Sims was very familiar with the helpless feeling, the worry over whether your child is going to live. Three years ago, he lost his 19 year old daughter to a skiing accident.

The Struggles of the Mind

The hay bales were like giant donuts in a place they did not belong. As far as you could see, they dotted the landscape. The cattle seemed to be more interested in the uncut hay than the neatly packaged bales cut for them. It was as if they were saving the baled hay for later. Stefan thought to himself, "They don't have a care in the world. Most likely, they don't fall in love. I have never heard of a cow with a broken heart." It had been over two years since Stefan had been home. He was always traveling to new cities, it was not uncommon for him to stay up until 2:00 am or 3:00 am in the morning working on projects. Therefore, home was a memory from his past for Stefan. One might wonder how he could overlook Christmas... well, just like he could miss his own birthday, Father's day and Valentine's Day. Some people are just comfortable with working all their lives. Stefan felt he finally understood the meaning of spending time with someone. He finally had a grasp on what the rest of his life could have been like, yet it was taken away.

The taste of cold lemonade on a hot day is something that everyone should experience at least once in his or her life. It is like a ray of sun on a winter day, but for Stefan, even Mom's lemonade could not bring a smile to his face. At least being home made it so he could breathe again and possibly even sleep.

Stefan's mom was an intelligent woman. She understood her son, so before she ever went to pick Stefan up from the hospital, she went into his room and took down any pictures of girls that he dated in high school or college. She closed the yearbooks and put away the family albums of the summers they spent at the lake with family and friends. She did not want anything to remind her son of the tragedy. She felt that Stefan needed a clean slate.

A Future Changed

Even though Bob, Stefan's father, always watched the 6:00 news and the 11:00 news, she told him, "When Stefan gets home, either watch it in your bedroom or not at all."
She was afraid that one of the TV stations would be running another episode about the tragedy at Eagle's Nest: The young architect who was unable to save his love from falling. The head of economic development for the city of Boston went on the news stating that they regrettably had to consider another architect because of deadlines they needed to meet. Though Stefan was their first choice, they were forced to search for another architect.

Most people would be thrilled to find their name on every newspaper and television station in America—but not Stefan—not for this reason. The publicity was associated with a terrible tragedy, a sad and haunting story. Stefan wanted to die. He wanted to hide away from everything. Only one thing kept Stefan alive... his love for Amanda. Every day he would think about her. Every time he closed his eyes, he would see her in his mind. He was madly in love with a woman that become a ghost only found in his dreams and thoughts.

A couple days had passed, and Stefan was at least walking

around. He would get up early in the morning, walk down the dirt road behind the house, and out into the pasture. Stefan looked at the hay bales; they were equally spaced across the rolling hills. He noticed the picket fence, how the tops pointed to heaven. The forest stuck out at the edge of the field like water along a beach. Tears filled his eyes because it all reminded him of Amanda. Although he saw those things as a child, he never took the time to look at them. His heart felt burdened because his thoughts were on Amanda. One morning when he was walking along the road, there was an empty Coca-Cola bottle on the ground. He picked it up; he did not think twice... a reflex, but a reflex, not of his—a reflex of hers. He never picked up a Coke bottle before, before Amanda he could have cared less. He figured a garbage man or a city worker would take care of it—somebody—but, not him. Now he tries to keep the world clean instinctively because of the time he spent with Amanda.

Time slowly moves

Amanda's mother and father stayed in a hotel across the street from Saint Anthony. It seemed they only used it to go shower and change clothes. Her mom slept in the chair next to Amanda's bed more than she slept at the hotel. It had been 72 hours, and today was the first meeting with both doctors since their initial evaluation to go over subsequent scans and progress. To be sure, Amanda's mom already asked many questions—she was in constant search for answers. She did not let a person leave Amanda's room without answering her latest questions.

Still, it was only basic stuff that was normal for a parent to ask, "What's that, how often, how does she look etc."

Doctor Hodgins looked concerned as he walked into the room and greeted the Wilsons.

"Doctor Sims will be running a little late; he is in surgery. Amanda is fighting as best as she can. I am surprised at her progress, everything I am seeing is better than expected. The swelling in the brain has gone down some. We were able to stop the internal bleeding, we have her right lung accepting air again, and it is almost back to capacity. The broken bones and skin grafts are doing fine."

The eyes of Amanda's mother filled with tears. She knew her daughter sustained many injuries but to hear them listed like a wall to climb was overwhelming. Doctor Hodgins stopped talking and put his hand on her knee,

"Mrs. Wilson there is no easy way to talk about her condition.

I have been doing this for twenty-nine years, and nothing has made it easier. Stay with me, we have not gotten to the major concerns yet. I need you to listen and understand the uphill battle Amanda is facing. While you are in the room with Amanda, she needs to hear you are strong when you talk to her, okay?"

She wiped the tears and apologized for getting emotional.

"You don't need to apologize for loving your daughter... Okay let's talk about her brain. We will not truly know the extent of brain activity until she is out of the coma. We still have a few more days until we feel it would be safe to bring her out of it."

Doctor Sims walked into the room and sat down at the table.

"Mrs. Wilson let me explain what is going on in your daughter's brain. The brain is an amazing part of the body. It is protected by a thick armor we call the skull. Though this protects it from everyday bumps and bruises, it cannot protect the brain against itself. Let me explain what I am talking about, look at this drawing of the brain inside the skull, you see that it fits with a small amount of space all around...a cushion if you will. If the brain receives a violent jolt, a sudden stop or impact against the skull the brain swells. A big danger from the swelling is that there is little room in this cavity for the brain to expand. The stem of the brain is a delicate section of the brain, if the swelling is too much it can press against the brain stem. This is a critical part of the brain; damage to this area can cause lifelong paralysis and even death. We are concerned because your daughter's brain is swollen due to the fall. We have her in an induced coma, which will help reduce the swelling. We also lowered her body temperature. Also known as therapeutic hypothermia, this too, will keep the swelling down. Usually, the inflammation from an injury peaks 48 to 72 hours post-injury, we are 72 hours in. We want to keep her cooled down for another three days before we bring her body temperature back up. We still have a long road ahead of us. Neither one of us believe in telling families the things you want to hear, rather what you need to hear. You need to keep praying. Keep talking to her; tell her everything is going to be all right. Tell her it is important that she rest. The less brain function right now the better. In a few days, we will start testing to see what we are dealing with."

Amanda's father pulled her mom close. He reached over to the doctor with an outstretched hand and said, "Thank you for all that you are doing."

Tears are common, though they come with a burden, they are part of the job. Even doctors cry, maybe not in front of patients or their families, but often behind closed doors they shed tears for the patients that have become like family to them. Amanda was still facing a very difficult road, but she was in the best hospital in the country.

Crumbling Walls

The phone was ringing off the hook at the houses of the Wilson's and Rogers. The media wanted interviews. Like sharks in a kiddy pool full of fish they could smell a juicy story and were circling. Fortunately, for the Rogers they lived in the country with a locked front gate that was a football field or two long. The Rogers, like the media, thought Amanda was dead. They had no idea Amanda was alive and fighting for her life. The media wanted the story told by Stefan, several news stations were offering in excess of a million dollars if he would talk. Hollywood directors sent letters; left messages on the phone with offers of more money than even Stefan could make throughout his whole career. His mother was starting to worry Stefan would find out they found Amanda's body. She took the phone off the hook, told Stefan there was a problem and a repairman was coming in a couple weeks to fix it. They were going to have the whole house re- wired, so it had to be scheduled in advance. The old Stefan, the healthy, clear-thinking Stefan would have caught her lie, it was a pretty lame one but, it was all she could think to say. Stefan did not notice, because he was so distraught over the loss of Amanda.

Every mom wants to protect her child from pain. It starts before she ever gives birth. Perhaps it started when she herself was a child. She felt what it was like to hurt and at that moment she swore to never let any child of hers go through that pain. Stefan's mom did everything she knew to do, she posted the property, unplugged the television, and hid the radios and phone. She was so worried Stefan was going to find out, she even had trouble sleeping. She was exhausted, just worn out. Around noon, Stefan had taken a walk in the back of the yard. He heard the props of a helicopter flying over the property. It seemed too close, he walked around to the front of the house and he saw the television station vans at the front gate. He stood there looking at them for a long time. In his gut he knew that something was going on, they were not there just to talk to him, there had to be a story. He went into the house; his mom was asleep, sitting in her chair by the fireplace. His father was back in the bedroom watching the news. Stefan called to his mom, but she did not answer. As he was walking towards her, he heard his name from his father's room.

"Stefan Rogers has not been seen since the body of Amanda Wilson was found. We believe that he is at his parents' house in the country."

The news anchor was solemnly sharing a picture of Stefan from the ribbon cutting ceremony at the falls, and in the background a picture of his parents' home taken from the helicopter which circled the property earlier. Then, they switched to a picture of Amanda, a college photograph of her smiling at graduation. The news reporter retold the whole story, showing Amanda, then Stefan, and finally Eagle's Nest.

Stefan started getting upset,

"Mom, Mom... she is gone, she died! They found her—she died! I had hopes; a part of me did not want to believe it was real. I thought one day she would be found..." Stefan sat down on the couch, "I thought if I did not ask about her, maybe God would let her live. What am I going to do Mom? I loved her so much."

They spent the rest of the day talking about God. Stefan was especially curious why his mother still believed in him even after her personal tragedies. Her parents died in a plane crash, his father experienced unspeakable horrors as a POW, and of course now the loss of Amanda. Stefan believed, but his faith was not as strong as his mom's, nor as strong as Amanda's.

"Mom I never talked to her parents... Her brother is going to be a mess. He is autistic."
  Stefan had trouble talking.

"She loved him so much, Mom. He used to sit by the door when she was coming home from college and wait for hours for her to arrive. He would say 'Manda coming... 'Manda coming.' over and over. When he was younger he had trouble saying the "A" in Amanda, so he calls her 'Manda. After sitting there for a long time, he would walk over to Amanda's mom, put his hand on her shoulder, and tell her 'Manda... coming, 'Manda... coming.' How is he going to deal with this, Mom?"

  For the first time, Stefan thought about the pain that others were going through. He walked outside and sat in the swing. His mom let him go. She did not want him to find out, but in a way, she was happy he was talking about it instead of retreating. She knew he had a long road ahead of him.

A Mother's Ear

He found himself sitting on the porch in the evening hours and watching the sun go down. Occasionally his mom would come out and sit with him. She was waiting to hear about the woman and the accident.

"Stefan, I know it's hard. I remember when my mom and dad died in the plane crash. I wanted to blame God, I was unhappy for months. I still have an emptiness in me that I cannot fill, I assure you when I get to Heaven, Stefan, I will have many questions for God.
The truth is, life does not stop. Sometimes to get over things, honey, you have to talk about them. You cannot keep them bottled up inside. I know that you're having a hard time with this. You're my baby. I can see it in your eyes. When you're ready to talk, I'm here."

Stefan wiped the tears from his eyes and continued to look at the sunset. The only noise was the crickets in the distance and the ice cubes melting and sliding down the side of the glass.

"She was the most amazing person I've ever met."

Stefan's mother felt as though her heartbeat stopped for a minute. They were finally at a point that Stefan was going to tell her what had happened and tell her about the woman that her son fell in love with. Before Stefan finished his first sentence, his mom's eyes filled with tears because she knew her son's heart was broken. She could hear it in the way he was talking and see it in the way his hands were twisting together like throwing away paper.

"You remember that project in Boston, the one by the building called The Falls?"
His mom nodded her head, reached over, and put her hand on his.

"Go ahead, Stefan."

"Well, Amanda was an environmental engineer hired by Boston to make sure the project was run cleanly."
He reached up with his free hand and wiped his eyes.

"Mom, you remember Suzy Toddler who used to live over off Lime?"

"Yeah, baby."

"You remember how I used to get all tongue-tied when I was talking to her?"

"Oh, you sure did. You couldn't say three words without messing them up."

"Well, that's how I felt around Amanda when I met her. I tried to talk to her, Mom, and I could not even speak. I tried to say 'Hello.' I just felt my heart beating in my chest. It beat so hard I thought she saw it."

She started patting his hand in confirmation.

"She was the most polite person I've ever met. She loved her job, but she loved nature more than anything else. I wanted you to meet her. The day I met her is the first time I ever wanted to bring someone home to meet you."

His mom smiled and squeezed his hand.

"Go on, baby. It's okay."

"So, I didn't know how she felt about me. I thought she cared. I thought I could see it in her eyes, hear it in her voice, but it wasn't until we took the trip to Eagle's Nest that things progressed, and we became closer. I realized I had fallen in love with her. That look Grandpa always had when he looked at Grandma, the way he held her hand…"

Stefan started crying. He couldn't talk anymore. He just said, "Mom."

She got up out of her chair, put her arms around him, and told him, "That's enough for now, Stefan. It's okay."

"You don't understand, Mom. I couldn't save her. I couldn't

save her."

He started crying and shaking his head.

His mom hugged him, squeezed him tight, and told him, "It'll get better. Just give it time. It'll get better."

A Beating Heart

Sitting next to Amanda, her mother thought of all the times as a little girl she lay in her arms and slept. A child nestled against her mother's bosom. Clearly, she felt safe against the beating heart of her mother. Maybe all we truly want in life is to be held, feel safe. Now her mother could only hold her hand and sit next to her. The days of tiny toes and spinning mobiles are gone. Now a mother sat next to her daughter, not as a shield of protection, but a comforting energy. She held her hand and told her how beautiful she was, how proud they were of the woman that she had become.

"I saw pictures of Stefan on the news... he is such a handsome young man. I know he is looking forward to seeing you. Everyone wants to hear about you two. Michael misses you, he asks about you every day."

Just then, they heard a beep from the heart monitor. Amanda's pulse had increased. Julie came into the room and checked the lines leading to the machine.
Amanda's mom asked,

"What is going on?"

Julie looked up from listening to Amanda's heart beat and asked,
"What were you talking about? What did you just tell her?"

Amanda's mom said, "I was talking about Stefan and how

much Michael missed her. What is going on?"

Julie called out to the other nurse at the station to page Doctors Sims and Hodgins *stat*. She turned to Amanda's mom and told her,

"Mrs. Wilson, can you please sit down over there, and the doctors will tell you what is going on in a minute...? Don't worry this is a good thing!"

Amanda's mom did not know whether to cry or smile, but she sat down as Julie asked. Two more nurses came into the room and started checking equipment.

Doctor Sims was the first to arrive. "What is going on Julie?"
"Doctor Sims, Amanda's heart beat reacted to her mother's conversation."

"Unbelievable, did you page Doctor Hodgins?"

"Yes, he is over in the north ER; he will be here in about 15 minutes."

"Mrs. Wilson, can we go into the next room to talk for a minute?"
   Amanda's mom was worried why Doctor Sims wanted to talk to her.
"Everything is okay, we just want to tell you what is going on."

She sat down on a bench. Doctor Sims acted as if he was not sure how to start the conversation, almost as if he was stalling. Just then, Doctor Hodgins walked in,

"Hello Mrs. Wilson, I hear we have some things to talk about."

"Please tell me what is going on, is it bad...? Did I do something wrong? Is she okay?"

"No, Mrs. Wilson, no, not at all. Amanda has not stopped surprising us. You remember we told you that we cooled her body and brain temperature down to help with swelling?"

"Yes..."

"Well during this time we rarely see an increase in heart rate... This can only mean a couple things, either she is dreaming, she is having internal issues of which we are not aware, or she is hearing you and is reacting to what you are telling her."

"Is that a good thing?"

"If she is reacting to your speech then that is a great thing, we just have not seen it from a patient in the state she is in. Amanda has broken all the rules so far... It is possible she has pulled herself out of the coma—or is at least trying. We have altered the medication to get her body temperature back to normal, but we need to find out why her heart beat increased."

Doctor Hodgins replied as he reached over and put his hand on her knee.

"We'll need you to talk to her again in about twenty minutes. We are going to let her system calm down, so we have a constant heart rate to measure."

"Did you see her eyes move?" doctor Sims asked.

"No, I—I don't know—I wasn't looking, I was just talking to her like I have been every day since she has been here."

"Just relax, everything is going to be okay, we will run the test in a few minutes. You might not want to call your husband until after we re-assess her. We do not want him to get excited if she is reacting for another reason..."

Twenty minutes does not sound like a long time, but if you are the parent of an ill child, twenty minutes can seem like an hour—if not more. Julie came to the door. Doctors, we are ready for you.

"Come on Mrs. Wilson, let's go find out what is happening."

Amanda's mom walked over and sat down by her bed. She started talking to Amanda just as she had earlier, but this time the room was full of specialists and doctors.

"Baby I had to step out for a bit, I am sorry. We know that you are going to be fine, even Tackle misses you."

Tackle was the family dog, given his name because when he was a puppy every time he ran towards her little brother, Michael would say "No tackle," so they named dog Tackle.

"Michael can't wait for you to come home, you know what he says, 'Sissy coming, Sissy coming,' just like he did when you were off to school and came home for the weekends."

There was a beep, then another... Doctor Sims whispered, "Damn, I don't believe it."

Her heartbeat clearly increased when her mom was talking about her brother.

Doctor Hodgins leaned down toward her mom and whispered in her ear, encouraging her to continue to talk to her, "Ask her if she can squeeze your hand."

Amanda's mom had tears in her eyes. She had trouble speaking; Doctor Hodgins put his hand on her shoulder.

"Amanda baby, if you can hear me, please squeeze my hand."

There was a long pause; the room was quiet except for the machines that monitored the things they could not see.

"Amanda, I know you can hear me, please baby squeeze my hand."

Then Doctor Sims saw the cord attached to her finger move, not much, but it moved.

"Tell her again!"
Both doctors were full of hope and anticipation, but nothing happened. Amanda's mom started to cry; she turned to the doctors and said,

"If Stefan was here I bet she would react."
Suddenly Amanda squeezed her mother's hand—her mother gasped aloud.

"Amanda, Amanda, baby I am here! I love you, I am here baby."
The doctors shook their heads; they watched as Amanda tried to squeeze her mother's hand. A squeeze, in most other circumstances, is really just movement of the fingers—nothing more. However, in Amanda's case, it meant not only could she hear but she also had the brain control to move her fingers.

"Amanda, this is Doctor Sims. You are at Saint Anthony's Hospital; can you open your eyes?
Eyes that had been shut for days twitched.
"That a girl, it's okay, everything is going to be okay."
Amanda's mom was holding her hand in both of hers. Tears were falling from her cheeks, "Come on baby, and open your eyes for us."

Then, as though she was a baby born in the dark of night, Amanda opened her eyes. She strained to see the world around her, but managed just enough to see the shapes in her room, the light and shadows of a new world.

Amanda's mom started talking to her, telling her how much she loved her. The doctors started ordering tests and procedures they didn't expect to be ordering for several days.

"We need this information right away." Doctor Hodgins told Julie.

"Amanda, you are at Saint Anthony's Hospital, you had a bad fall. Do you remember? Don't try to speak just close your eyes... for yes."
Amanda slowly closed her eyes... no one in the room could stand still, they were like children waiting for ice cream.

"Amanda, Stefan is fine; you are going to be okay. We are going to run some tests; everything is going to be all right."

Doctor Sims told Julie,
"I want a CT scan, a brain wave test and blood work to be done right away. I want to be paged as soon as they are finished."

The room was full of people moving equipment, like a busy city street. But, the one thing that stayed constant was Amanda's mother sitting by her side, holding her hand. Amanda started to cry, tears ran down the sides of her face. Her mother reached over and wiped them off.

"I love you so much baby, we have all been praying for you...God is so good."

Stefan Decides to Leave

That night at supper, there was not much conversation. Stefan ate, but he did not eat much and his father was never much for words. Nevertheless, a comment escaped that perhaps no one in the room was ready to hear.

"Stefan, don't you think it's about time for you to get back to work?"

Stefan's mom looked at her husband, looked at the father of her hurting child. It was an angry look, a look of disbelief. The look you give someone before you never speak to him or her again. She was giving that look to Stefan's father.

Stefan looked up at his mom and then looked at his dad. "I'm not going back."

His dad wiped his mouth with a napkin and put it back on his lap. He put his elbows on the table and looked at Stefan. "What are you going to do, son? Things happen in life. You've got to move on."

"I've got some things I've got to do first, Dad. I cannot just walk away. I've got to go back to Eagle's Nest and face what happened."

His mom quickly reached over, grabbed his hand, and said, "Son, you don't need to go back there. We know what happened; you know what happened. You do not need to take yourself back there. You don't need to face that again."

Stefan said, "No, Mom. I have to. You see, I died with her, and maybe if I go back..."
He could not finish the sentence. He started crying, stood up, and walked away from the table.

His father whispered, "Oh hell."

His mom stood up, pushed her husband's arm,
"The war did more damage than you will ever realize."

She followed Stefan out of the room. Stefan was sitting on the porch. The stars were out. The silhouettes of the hay bales loomed in the distance.

"Stefan, I don't think it's a good idea for you to go back there."

"Mom, you've got to let me go. It's something I have to do. I don't know anything anymore, It should have been me—not her—who died that day."

She pleaded, "Well, let me go with you. I'll take you."

"No, Mom. I need to go by myself. I need to be alone. I need to find out who I am and what I believe in."

If anything, Stefan was driven and his mom knew it. Facing a terrible tragedy was not going to suddenly make him stop being stubborn.

Reluctantly, she conceded, "Okay, if you're going to go, I understand, but I need you to get some sleep before you go. I do not want you leaving tonight. Get a good night's rest, eat a hearty breakfast, and then we'll get you packed up in the morning. I wish you'd let me go with you, but I suppose you know what's best."

Stefan gave her a hug—a deep hug, held her tightly, kissed the side of her face, and nodded his head. Then he went through the screen door back to his old bedroom and laid down.

Losing Him Again

Stefan awoke mid-morning and went into the kitchen. His mom had breakfast waiting—relatively simple—eggs, bacon, and toast. Memories came flooding in… the care-free days of high school—college breaks, the smell of bacon in the morning and his mom's sweet voice tirelessly telling him everything would be all right. She always asked him about his life, what he wanted to do—what hurdle he would jump next.

Stefan's family was driven. His father spent time in Vietnam, in the army. When he came home, he was a hard worker and provided for his family the best he could. His mother was a very loving woman, very compassionate, and very religious. She believed there was nothing that happened in life that God did not know about. She did not believe God was the cause of everything. She felt life had its own course, free will, and many times even God cried due to its outcome.

Stefan did not say much; there was no better cook than his mom. His father came in, and before he could sit down, Stefan's mom poured him a cup of coffee and laid the newspaper to the right side of the plate as she had for the last thirty years.

His father sat there and looked at Stefan, "You sure you know what you're doing, son?"

"Yeah, Dad. I do. I've got to find some answers."

"Well, you know that job in Boston is an important job."

And all of a sudden, his father felt the backhand of his mom. "Stay out of it, Bob. It's none of your business. He'll be all right. He can always go back and be an architect whenever he wants. You need to stay out of it."

Stefan could tell by the tone of her voice that his mom was serious. Even the man who had spent five years in Vietnam knew not to mess with her. She was religious, compassionate, and loving, but she was also a very powerful woman when she wanted to be. She would not take no for an answer if it was important to her. The last thing she wanted to hear right now was Stefan's father drilling him about his career. Stefan needed space, find the answers to what was next.

As always, Stefan's mom packed him a lunch. Just like every time he headed off to college, his mom would pack him a lunch so he could save a couple dollars for gas. Stefan smiled and gave his mom a big hug; he had tears in his eyes.

"I don't know when I'm coming home. I guess when I find the answers."

Her eyes filled with tears because she knew her son was hurting and knew that the only way he would move on was to face the tragedy head on. Stefan had never backed down from a challenge—had never backed down from adversity. He was always willing to face problems head on, but this was more than a problem. This was his heart, a heart now torn in two. The very fibers of his belief were in question, and she honestly did not know if he would ever recover.

His dad stood up and shook his hand. Then he reached over, pulled him to his chest and patted him on the back. Stefan was shocked. The only other time he ever did that was when Stefan won a national architect award in college in front of an auditorium of ten thousand people. Maybe it was the war, or maybe it just was how he was raised? His father was just not a guy that showed his emotions.

A Hard Goodbye

Stefan cleared his throat, turned and gave his mom a half wave, and then he headed out the screen door. He walked out the gravel driveway to his car, stood there for a moment looking over the pasture of hay; He knew it would be the last time that he saw it. You see, what Stefan did not tell his mom or dad is that he was not coming back. He was leaving this world to be with Amanda. He would go to the spot where he failed to keep her alive and give his life to try to find her in the afterworld. Some people would say that he passed the point of rational thinking. He was walking away from one of the biggest architectural jobs in the United States, national media's attention, and yet Stefan—rational, logical Stefan—had checked out. The city of Boston had already made an announcement that, unfortunately, regrettably, and with great sympathy, they had to turn the project over to another architect. Stefan did not even notice. In fact, he had not thought about the project ever since the accident. His only thoughts had been of Amanda. His only concern was how he was going to get back to her.

It had been four weeks since the accident and Stefan still had not recovered. He still saw her every night when he closed his eyes and he still felt her hand slipping from his. Even though Stefan liked music and would always listen on road trips, now was not a time to sing along. He put on The Four Seasons, Mozart and Yo-Yo Ma and listened to the strings vibrate in the air as he headed north.

It was a good four-hour drive, plenty of time for self-reflection, plenty of time to remember all of the special moments with Amanda. Like most relationships, the physical was one of the most powerful memories. He could smell her skin. He could taste her lips; feel her breasts against his chest, the heartbeat that vibrated into his body. Stefan was madly in love with her. Tears rolled down the sides of his face. The passion and chemistry between them was not something easily forgotten, but there was so much more to Amanda than just the physical relationship. There was the spiritual, the emotional, the energy he never felt with another person. He could hear her laughter and see her smile. As he headed north, the mountain terrain became steeper. He felt his heartbeat increase, felt sure it was the fact he was getting closer to where Amanda was.

A Table for One

He stopped at the same restaurant where Amanda and he had stopped a month ago. He noticed the old dog was not on the porch. He went inside, the waitress asked to seat him. He looked over and saw a couple sitting by the window where Amanda and he once sat.

He told the waitress, "I'll wait until that table is available."

"That's fine."

"How are you doing?"

He said, "Fine. Thank you."

Tears started forming in her eyes,   "I'd better get back to the kitchen."

He said, "Okay."

The accident was not a secret to the world. Every detail of Stefan and Amanda's story was broadcasted on all of the television stations. It was a tragic, tragic event. The waitress actually recognized Stefan from their visit and the constant posting of his image on the news.

The lobby of the country restaurant, which is really just an opening next to the front door, had all wooden chairs, none of them the same. They looked like they were ancient family heirlooms—shared from each generation to the next generation. As he sat there and watched the young couple laugh and smile, he had to think about Amanda and the lunches they had, the view of the river in the distance—how perfect everything was only a month or two ago. He slowly wiped the tears from the corners of his eyes trying not to draw any attention to emotions. He sniffed in slowly, which is hard to do when the tear ducts are flowing.

The couple finished their meal and the waitress started cleaning the table. Before she was done, Stefan was already sitting down. He was sitting in the same chair, facing the same way. He took out his phone and turned to the picture of her sitting across from him that he had taken their first meal. He laid it on the table, closed his eyes, and she was there.

The waitress went and got him a glass of water. She was not composed enough to ask him if he was hungry or wanted anything to eat.   She figured at least he could bring him a glass of water. She could sense that he was on a journey, his visit was more than just stopping in to eat. He sat there silent, no less than a man at the grave.

After twenty minutes of Stefan staring out the window, the waitress came back and asked him, "Sir, would you like something to eat?"

Stefan looked at her and said, "I'm not hungry. Thank you."

Normally she would have asked him to move to a single chair table because, in small towns, you don't make any money unless people are coming and going – normally the waitresses kind of get insistent that you move on. If you're not buying anything they're not making any money, but she sat down across from Stefan and reached over and put her hands on his. She said, "I'm sorry."

He looked at her with tears dropping to the table and said, "Me too. It was my fault...I—couldn't save her."

The waitress put her hand on her mouth, tears rolling down her face and said, "Oh my God, how could you think it was your fault? Honey, it was an accident. God, it was just an accident. These mountains take the lives of people every year. You had no way of stopping what happened. You've got to believe that."

Stefan was looking out the window. As his tears were dropping to the table, he did not say a word. For the longest time, the waitress sat there holding his hands. Even the owner of the restaurant was moved. She was not worry about the loss of a table. She saw that it was Stefan.   A short lady that had been cooking southern fried meals all her life, came over and put her arm on his back and told him, "Darling', ain't nobody can take that burden from yea, but you're going to be alright. I assure yea, you're going to be alright."

Stefan could feel the warmth of her hand and the hand of the waitress. Though he was alone, he could feel the compassion. And his response, he just nodded as he looked out the window.

They sat for a short while longer and then Stefan told them it was time for him to move on. When he stood up, the waitress gave him a hug, a deep hug, a compassionate hug—a hug she wished could have been from Amanda to him.

And she whispered in his ear, "It's not your fault, Stefan. It's not your fault."

He was shaking, though his eyes could no longer produce tears he clearly was hurting. They were as red as they could be and his heart was as broken as any man's heart could ever be.

By the time the waitress let go, the owner grabbed him and wrapped her arms around him, strong, almost like a bear hug, like a man, but sensitive and compassionate.

Stefan told them, "Thank you so much. I need to get going...What happened to the old dog that used to sit out front?"

"Hun, He died about a month ago."

"I am sorry to hear that," Stefan said.

He put 15 dollars on the table for a glass of water, but that is just how Stefan was. He turned and slowly walked out the door.

Clouds in a Blue Sky

It was winter now, and the skies were a crisp, bright blue, holding promise of good things to come. But, for Amanda's parents, the blue skies were clouding over as their concern deepened. Amanda had slowly shown signs of improvement since being brought to the trauma unit. Even though her parents were hopeful, they knew there were still issues. Their daughter would or could only move her had back and forth at times, and she would squeeze her parents' hands in recognition. They silently worried that Amanda's condition would remain permanent, but neither of them would say it out loud.

They were also struggling with the fact that they had left Amanda's brother with family, and he needed them as well. They told him they had to help a family member who was ill and needed them. He seemed to grasp the idea and was okay with it, but they knew he did not like change. Thinking ahead to what may happen or could happen, they knew it would be a difficult to explain it to their son. Indeed, the blue skies held some clouds.

Amanda still could not talk and was only moving her head a little to the right and left. Doctor Sims and Hodgins called the Wilson's in for a consult to hear progress.

"It is a great sign that she has opened her eyes and is able to squeeze your hand. You need to understand that we are not on a sure path to recovery yet. The test came back, and the neurologist is telling us there is still a large amount of swelling in her lower back. Unfortunately, she is still not showing any signs of moving her toes. Please do not jump to any conclusions to what this means...other than it is a concern. Everything that your daughter does in the next few months will give us more clues as to the damage that she has suffered and if she will be able to walk again." Doctor Sims told them.

"Mr. & Mrs. Wilson I want to tell you I believe that everything is going to work out for Amanda, but I can't. It is not my job as her doctor to make you feel better but to give you the facts. She still is fighting to survive everyday. We still have not gotten her collapsed lung back to capacity. The broken bones seem to be healing, she is going to need to be in rehab for a long time. I believe that until we know all her internal issues, you should not tell Michael that she is alive or recovering. I am not concern about society, I am concerned that she has not turned the corner yet. I am sorry I do not want to give you false hope or cause Michael to lose his sister twice. Please do not miss understand me it is great her eyes are open, the fact that she squeezed your hand but beyond that we have to wait for the swelling to go down and see how much damage to her brain if any has accord.

Amanda's parents listened to everything the doctor was telling them, holding each other's hand tightly, fighting back the tears that came with a troubled heart. This news was not what they anticipated. They wanted to hear that Amanda was going to be okay. Maybe in a week or two, she could transfer out of ICU and into a room where family and friends could visit, that's the news they were hoping for. It is heart wrenching for a mother to hope and pray everyday that her child does not die—knowing there is nothing she can do. During the night will she get a call that Amanda is no longer with us? It was all overwhelming, draining emotionally and mentally.

"Tell us what we can do. You will let us know when we can tell Michael... when she is safe... right?"

"Absolutely... I know your heart; I have been there. You will be the first person I call if there is a change in her condition. I would love to tell you only good news but I have to be honest with you because you need to know the truth.   Listen your daughter reminds me of mine. I will do everything I possibly can to help her make it through this." Doctors Sims said as he was holding the hand of Amanda's mom.

Back on Track

Stefan turned around and walked back into the restaurant and asked Mary Lou where City Hall was and how would he find out property taxes. She told him to go down 771 and take a left on Brewer and go about a mile, and the buildings on the right were the public offices for the town.

Stefan took her by the hand and told her, "Thank you," and once again headed out the door.

It was 3:00 in the afternoon before he got to the tax office. He showed them the address of the cabin that he had stayed in with Amanda. He requested the name and phone number of the owner. Bobbie Jo was a nineteen-year-old girl that loved mystery novels and romance. There was not a person in Long Ridge that did not know of the death of Amanda. Everyone knew the story, so when he said his name, Bobbie Jo knew Stefan; she noticed his eyes were red from tears. She knew that he had been crying. Clearly still upset over the accident. "What address are you trying to find there, sweetie?" Bobbie Jo said.

"I'd like the phone number of the owner of this cabin up near Eagle's Nest."

"Well, I'm sure if he's paying taxes I'll find it here in our records. Now we ain't got computers, but we're pretty good at keeping records."

So Bobbie Jo looked through her file and after a ten-minute search, she found the owner Samantha Becker.

Buying the Cabin

Samantha Becker lived in California, but she inherited the cabin from her uncle. It was something that she used as a place to go play—to get away from city life and view the mountains. The cabin really was not worth much, maybe 60,000 dollars. However, she could not otherwise afford a vacation home.

Stefan asked Bobbie Jo, "Do you have a phone that I can use, my cell phone is dead?"

Bobby Jo point in the direction of a room that clearly had not been used in a long time. "Right through there is a phone on that desk. Ain't nobody used that office in years. It is just storage now."

Stefan cut her off a little short and said, "Thank you. Can you give me a minute please?"

Stefan sat down at a desk. There was more dust than paper, a room with one light bulb, like you would see in the old movies…like an interrogation room. He dialed Samantha's number. He was pleasantly surprised when Samantha answered. She was a hairstylist and had her own little boutique.

"This is Samantha, 'Your Designs.' How can I help you?"

Stefan said, "My name is Stefan Rogers."

Before he could get out another word, Samantha started to cry.

"Stefan, I know who you are... I'm so sorry, I'm so sorry."

Stefan was not good at hiding his feelings, his voice became broken as he spoke. Though he had heard sympathy from everyone that he seemed to meet, he still choked up when he felt the compassion.

He said, "Samantha, I was wondering if you wouldn't mind—I mean, would you consider selling me the cabin?"

Samantha said, "Oh gosh, Stefan. I don't know. It's been in my family..."

Before she finished her sentence, he blurted out,

"I'll give you $100,000."

"Stefan, that's a lot of money..."

"$150,000, Samantha."

Samantha said, "Stefan, you're hurting right now and you're not making a rational decision. Take some time and think about it."

"I don't want to think about it. I'll wire you the money tomorrow."

Samantha said, "There's not much in the cabin."

"I don't care. I'll take whatever is in it. If there's something you want I'll box it up and ship it to you, Samantha I need the cabin."

Stefan asked Samantha if she would allow him to go ahead and move in since he was there—sleep there tonight and she said,

"Absolutely. No problem. Everything's turned on."

"Don't worry about it. I'll have everything switched over after we close the sale. And again, if you can think of anything you want out of the house Samantha, I'll be more than happy to ship it to you."

Samantha knew that the money would help her. It would get her back in the black, and she would have plenty of money left over to buy another place that would be closer, less expensive for her weekend getaways. She told Stefan that she'd have the contract drawn up tomorrow and ship it to him.

Stefan asked Bobbie Jo, where the nearest real estate office was.

She said, "There ain't no office, but my daddy, he's got a real estate license."

"That's fine. I just need him to be able to do some paperwork for me. I'm going to buy Samantha's property."

Bobbie Jo said, "Stefan, you'll love that place. It's a beautiful place."

Stefan turned to her and said, "I know, I'll see you tomorrow. If you could have your father give me a call, here's my phone number."

Bobbie Jo took his card, put her hand on top of his hand, and held it tight. He pulled it away slowly and walked towards the door.

Back to a Dream

Stefan pulled into the yard of the cabin, turned the engine off and sat there. It was like going back in time. He could still hear her voice, her laughter as tickling her before they got out of the car. It all flashed back. It was like watching a home movie except there was no screen. His eyes were open, but he was not looking ahead. He was looking into his memory. It seemed fifteen minutes, twenty minutes before he ever got out of the car and made his way up to the cabin. A slow motion movie, Amanda walking in front of him... never close enough to touch. He looked at the kitchen and he saw her standing there cutting the vegetables. He walked down the hallway towards the bedroom, he remembered twisting and turning, rolling against the wall, making out before they reached the bedroom. It was hard for Stefan to be there, but he knew he would find answers. He believed if he felt her presence, then it would be easier for him to end his own life. If he spent enough time in the cabin before going up to Eagle's Nest, then stepping off the edge would only be like stepping into a dream to be by her side.

Stefan did not cook a fancy meal. In fact, he bought some sandwiches from the gas station. The only meal Stefan had with him was what his mother had packed away in the cooler. It was always enough and probably even more than enough. On top of that, he was not hungry—had no intent on enjoying a meal. He really felt he was there for one purpose only. He was there to evaluate the value of his life, to step across into eternity to find Amanda. He figured the best way to do it would be to spend time in every place that they had been.

About 11:30, 12:00 he finally fell asleep. His dreams lately have always been about her. Seldom does he have a dream that she is not included. This time he dreamed that he was fishing on a calm lake and nothing was biting. Then he saw Amanda standing at the shore waving at him. He paddled over and picked her up, called her his lucky charm. He took her to the center of the lake and caught more fish than he had ever caught before. She never said a word. She just sat there smiling. All his dreams somehow encompassed Amanda. She was always part of them now.

The next morning Stefan went downtown and completed the paperwork for the purchase of the home. He made a lot of money off the design of The Falls so, there was not really a need for him to work for a few years. He had saved his money since he was a child. He was not a guy who went out and bought fancy cars. He wore classy clothes, but he lived in the city, so he always took taxis everywhere he went. There was no need to have a sports car to impress. Even the wealthiest people in the city took taxis. Therefore, he still had a very large sum of money stashed away, so $150,000 had little meaning to him. It was a mere dent out of his pile. He wired the money to Samantha along with a thank you letter via text.

Holding on to Hope

Amanda was not getting worse, but she was not getting better as quickly as her parents had hoped. They had been separated from Michael for over a week. They decided that Amanda's mom would go home for a couple days to be with Michael. He was having a terrible time, but his mom and dad were doing what they thought was best by not telling him that she was alive. If he found out she was alive, and then she "died again," it would be devastating. Parents do not always make the right choices; not everyone agreed, but it was their daughter and son. Over the years advice about raising an autistic child came from many sources, most of them clueless. Twenty-four hours a day for 8 years gave them a concrete understanding of what their son could handle. Amanda's mom was worried and felt she needed to go see Michael; her maternal instincts told her he needed to see his mom. Julie overheard the parents talking. In college, she interned at a doctor's office that specialized in children like Michael, so this touched Julie more than normal.

An hour later Julie entered the room with Jim Patterson from SkyVac,
"Mr. and Mrs. Wilson this is Jim Patterson from SkyVac, he is the commander of the search and rescue crew that found your daughter.

Mr. Wilson had tears in his eyes, he did not reach out his hand, but instead he hugged Jim. Mrs. Wilson did the same.

"Julie called me and told me about your need to spend time with Michael, I know that you live 3 hours from here. I would like to help your family. I own four helicopters; I would like you to allow me to taxi you from here to there anytime you need to visit Michael. This will save you four hours of windshield time."

It was an amazing act of kindness from a man that saved their daughters life...Everyone in the room had tears in their eyes.

The kindness of Jim and the fact that Julie cared enough to make the phone call was overwhelming for the Wilsons.

"If you want, my daughter is an occupational therapist, and I am sure she will be more than happy to help with Michael if you want to bring him to the hotel to stay in town. We all know this is a tremendous burden on your family, and the least we can do is help you in any way we can."

Jim's offer would give them a chance to visit Michael more with limited time away from the hospital. The offer to provide much needed respite at the hotel so Michael could stay with them caused Betty, Amanda's mom, eyes to fill with tears. Of course, for Michael it would be a trip out of town, nothing more than site-seeing. He loved trains and tall buildings stacked next to each other. The Wilsons were speechless.

A Dream of Tears

Stefan made the purchase. When he got back to the cabin and pulled into the yard, his eyes filled with tears. He could remember the smile on Amanda's face. He could remember holding her hand, walking around, and looking at the property. He was numb. He felt like passing out. He had trouble walking, he was in a daze. Like an alcoholic who had too much to drink, he stumbled. He walked straight through the house out the sliding doors back to the balcony. It was as though he was retracing the steps he had taken with Amanda. It was as if she was walking with him. He stood on the balcony and looked at the landscape. Tears fell like rain. There was no time. He did not know how long he stood there. Time did not exist. All he knew was that a woman he was terribly in love with died tragically and he was faced with that, faced with wondering every day what he could have done differently—seeing her face and feeling her hand slip out of his... hearing her desperate scream as the rain fell.

He walked back into the house and then into the kitchen. He remembered cutting up the vegetables. Although it happened over a month ago, it was as if they were still there, as if she was in the next room and this was all a terrible dream. Perhaps, he had fallen asleep that night and just had not awoken. Then this would be a terrible dream, a nightmare from which he would awaken and hold her tight, tell her that he loved her.

He walked back to the bedroom. He stood in the door, leaned against the frame and looked at the bed. Flashes of them making love with their hands against the wall, sweat running down her face, hair wet and eyes soft. Her smiling, biting her lip as she held onto his shoulders. The hours making love, lying naked together—everywhere he looked there were memories. Even the hall to the bedroom, against the wall he held her, kissing her deeply, knowing that just a few feet away they would make love. He would be with the woman he now only saw in his dreams.

He went back out to the dining room table and sat down. The burnt candle was half its original height. Though there was no fire on its wick tonight, it still reminded him of the night they ate supper, the wine spill—the heart pounding and the warmth of the skin. He did not call out her name in some delusional search. Stefan was distraught and angry at life, but he was not delusional. He could hear her voice in his head, her whisper. As he sat there, the tears piled on the table. So much so, it looked like a spilled glass of water. He squeezed his hands together below his chin. Some of his feelings were from desperately missing her, some were just sheer anger. Anger at God, life, everything he could not understand.

WHY

Only two months ago, he had the world, more money than any man his age could imagine, more fame than he could ever want, but she replaced it all—the love of a woman, so deep and so pure that nothing in life mattered. Fame, fortune, it was all just part of a past life void of love. It was the reality of what true love brings, and Stefan had it with Amanda. He had it not only in his hands, but also in his arms... not only in his arms, but also in his soul. He saw it in her eyes. She didn't have to say a word. He saw how much she loved him.

He spent the rest of the night sitting on the couch with only one light on. Some people call it staring, but in reality, he was daydreaming. He was daydreaming about all the events that led up to that weekend. Occasionally he would feel a shiver because he would think about the last hours and the last moments of her life - something he could not get out of his head.

He got up, went over, and took another pill and another one. Anything to help him sleep, but the problem with sleeping is you dream. The problem with dreaming is eventually you wake up alone.

Drops of Sand

Amanda's mother was walking towards her room when she saw Julie run into Amanda's room. Her heart dropped; she could tell by the activity that something was wrong. Then she heard,
"Doctor Sims to ICU 4; Doctor Sims to ICU 4."

That was Amanda's room! Her mother started walking faster; yet before she reached the door, Julie met her in the hall.

Julie saw Betty Wilson walking towards the room. Julie put her arms around her and led her to the private consultation room.

"Hey Betty, listen, your phone went into voice mail, we called your husband, Mike is on his way. We are not allowing anyone in the room at the moment. Amanda's temperature has spiked. She has not opened her eyes since last night. We have her downstairs getting scans." The hospital chaplain walked up; Betty's eyes filled with tears. The shock, the flooding of emotions filled her heart; she slowly sat down. "Betty, Father Steven is just here to comfort you until Mike shows up. I have to get back to her room."

"I have to see her, Julie you have to let me see my baby."

"Betty, she is down stairs in radiology having scans done, and she will be back in about twenty minutes, I promise—as soon as I can I will get you in there. Mike will be here shortly, as soon as we know what is going on, the doctors or I will come get you."

It Was Time

It was a beautiful morning in the mountains; even Stefan realized the beauty that existed around him, though his world was seemingly over. He gathered his clothes together, and was ready to go. He sat at the table and began to share his heart with his mother in a letter.

Dear Mom,

The first thing I need to tell you is that I had the greatest mom in the world. Never once, as a child did I feel unloved. Never once growing up did I feel I could not come to you when tragedies happened in my life. But Mom, this is a tragedy that even your loving arms cannot help. This is something that has taken my life, though I breathe. You and Dad have always been there for me, you've always understood my passions and desires in life. I need to let you know that I love you both as much as a human can love another, but I can't go on. I cannot continue to breathe air when my lungs are empty. My heart cannot continue to beat when it is still.

I loved her. I watched her die. I could not hold onto her. The one man in the world that she believed in, let her down. I could not save her, so how can I save myself? I am going to be with her. If there is not an afterlife, then I would still choose this because I would have lived every day thinking of her and wishing she was here. Therefore, either way, my choice to leave this earth is mine. It is my option—the only option—that is viable for my survival. Today I will go to Eagle's Nest, and I will be with her. I will miss you and Dad. Please know that I love you, but I cannot live life if I am already dead inside.

I will always love you,

Stefan

As he wrote his name, tears dropped onto the page staining the ink. He sat a minute, looked around the room and then finally he said to himself, "Now we wait for the rain."

He pushed the chairs in around the table. He stood there for a moment and smiled.   Something he had not done in days, weeks, not since the accident... He did not smile because of what he was fixing to do or that writing the letter had made him smile. He smiled because he pushed the chair in. He just wrote his mom a suicide letter, set the ground work to step off Eagle's Nest to be with Amanda, but because how meticulous he was, he was sure to push all the chairs in around the table before he left. The smile was short-lived; replacing it was the reality of his decision.

He climbed into his car and sat there. He turned the engine on and then he realized there were other things he needed to set in place. So he emailed his accountant to let Beth know that if something happened to him she was to go ahead and enact his will to move the monies into the accounts he had designated to protect his finances away from the government upon his death. Then Stefan took his phone and turned it off.

A Cracked Mirror

Stefan wiped the tears from his eyes, put his seat-belt on, and sat there looking at the house. He started backing down the beautiful drive to the main road. A life that could have been very different, a future that was full of amazing things, all changed in a matter of days and hours.

He pulled onto the main interstate and headed north. The drive was a reflection of life, not a joyous trip centered on family events. He just had random thoughts: birthday parties, weddings, pictures of his father coming home from Vietnam, his graduation from college, the day he won his first architectural bid, the ribbon cutting for The Falls. Things that any person would look back on their life as special events. Most people used those thoughts to change their mind about suicide, think twice about giving up. Nevertheless, Stefan had no desire to continue living.

He made it to Eagle's Nest. He had a bottle of water in his car, just enough to get him there, so he would not be dehydrated. He knew he would have a rigorous climb to where the accident happened. He wanted to leave the earth in the same place and in the same manner as Amanda. He felt it was only fitting that if he could not save her from a terrible death, then he would give himself to that terrible death. If there was a God then such devotion should evoke his compassion.

Growing up, he was taught that if you commit suicide you go to hell. Stefan did not care. All his logic, all his thinking in life, all his planning, and all his perfection could not prepare him for the realization that in the rarity of life he would find his soul mate. Yet he would also see her lose her life, feel her hand slip out of his and watch her fall to her death. It was beyond the comprehension of any human being to expect any man or any woman to be able to deal with such a tragedy.

Stefan sees Amanda

He reached the edge of the rock face. He was fixing to start his climb when he saw Amanda. She was standing at the edge of the mountain in the shadows of the rocks. Stefan stared. He did not know what to think. He cried out,

"Amanda!" She did not answer. He moved toward her as fast as he could and then he realized it was not her. It was a rock shaped like her, the physical form of her head, shoulders, and part of her side. He sat there looking at it, amazed. The facial structures were not there, a lot of the detail, but from a distance, in the shadows, it was Amanda.

Stefan could not move forward. The basic shape of the rocks mesmerized him, and for a moment—just a moment he felt like he was with her. He felt connected to her again. For the last month, he felt as if he was in hell. For the first time, he could take a breath. He felt close to her as though she was still with him.   He felt such an awakening from the shape of the rock that an idea came into his head. He was making a "Change Order" for his project. A "Change Order" is when a planned project has a change upon which everyone agrees. It is a do-over or an ending that was not in the original plan. This was a big change order for Stefan. He now was planning on doing a sculpture of Amanda so the whole world could see how beautiful she was, like a gravestone or burial mask... but this would be a life size Amanda. What if he could sculpt her perfectly? How much more of the feeling inside him would come back if he could take that rock and make it look just like her?

An architect has to be an artist to be good at what he or she does. Stefan was an incredible artist. Instead of spending his time sculpting, painting, or drawing, he spent it in a combination of mediums to make the buildings he designed a reality.

He walked back to his car and for the moment he set aside ending his life. The agony was still there the desire to be with Amanda caused his heart to hurt but he felt if he could sculpt Amanda at the edge of Eagle's Nest, then the world would see her as he did. People would come just to see the beautiful woman the architect tragically lost. They would understand why he jumped from that very spot to be with her. If young couples came there and saw her they would take the time to love each other more, commit to each other in deeper ways. Therefore, he felt that he had a calling, a responsibility, and a job to do before he went to see Amanda. Stefan started walking back to the car. Something was wrong—his vision became blurred and his head began to hurt. He reached out for the nearest tree to hold himself up. The pain in his head was so intense he had tears in his eyes. It was like a migraine that was crushing his skull, but Stefan had never had migraines. After a long period, his vision came back, but his head was still hurting. It felt as though something struck him so hard that it caused his vision to fade. He had no plans to see a doctor. After all, in a few days he was planning to leave this world anyway

Smiles are Gone

Amanda was fighting for her life. The doctors could not tell by her temperature and outward symptoms what was going on inside her. The years of working with fall victims had taught the doctors always to consider head and spinal issues first. Broken bones normally do not cause extreme issues. Of course, infections and extreme compound brakes are different. Doctors Sims and Hodgins were puzzled and concerned. They went to the consultation room and turned on the monitors. They called down to the scan room to send up the data. The screens lit up; Amanda's chest cavity and her brain showed up on different screens. As though looking at a 3D animated character, the doctors could see all of her body parts. The room was quiet; Julie stepped in and closed the door behind her.

"Mr. and Mrs. Wilson are in the waiting room... can you tell them what is going on?"

"It does not look good...she is swelling in the left hemisphere. I think she is trying to fight it, but if we can't get it figured out soon—she is not going to make it. I was worried about this, she has been through so much." Doctor Sims told Julie.

"I am afraid that our only option is to induce a coma again; this time let's hope her system reacts better. Maybe we should have kept her mother out of the room. Honestly I think we need to tell her not to talk to her at all for a few days. We need her brain activity to calm down. I believe hearing about Stefan and her brother brought her back too soon." Doctor Hodgins explained to Julie.

"Julie, go get the Wilson's and bring them in."

Moments passed, and Betty and Mike walked through the door.

"I wanted you to see what is going in inside of your daughter. We normally do not allow parents or loved ones into this room, but we feel you need to see what we are looking at to understand what we are going to ask of you and what is next for Amanda."

Betty and Mike looked at the images of their daughter and were amazed at the technology. Unfortunately, the technology also showed things that were hard to see. The broken bones, the lung that was still trying to work correctly. The images were the best in the country; they could see her beating heart as clearly as if it were in the palms of their hands.

"Look, you see this area of the brain? This controls emotions; we believe thought is derived from this section. It is like the television, without it nothing can be seen. We believe it is swelling because the damage from the fall has not healed and she got too excited about hearing your voice, but especially from hearing about Michael and Stefan. Mr. And Mrs. Wilson we need to put her back into a coma, it is the only way to try and reduce this swelling and limit the chance of permanent damage or sudden death. We are fighting for her life every day. I know she is trying, but we have to help her."

Betty had tears rolling down the side of her face.

"Listen Mrs. Wilson, I know you love her, but for now she needs to have no emotions. Let her dream of whatever, but if she hears your voice, or hears about Stefan or Michael it might cause her to fight to wake up, which could put her life in danger. Please understand we are on the edge of life right now. To be perfectly honest, she is fighting every second to stay with us. I need you to follow my rules, can you do that?"

Mrs. Wilson's heart was broken, her daughter could die any minute, yet she could not tell her she loved her. She was a smart woman and understood that the sound of her voice could cause her to fight to wake up. The last thing they wanted was for Amanda to wake up before she was ready.

"How long? How long will we have to wait?"

"Mrs. Wilson I can't answer that—a week, a month, maybe two months. All I can tell you is that every day she is alive it gets her a little closer to getting better. Her lung gets stronger; the blood becomes richer, and by the grace of God the swelling goes back down. Please, I know you have been through a lot, and what I am asking of you may seem difficult or cruel, but I am trying to be as flexible as I can with your needs as a mother and mine as her physician. Please understand, I know you love her."

Betty wiped the tears from her eyes and told the doctors that Amanda is a fighter, and she was going to be alright. Mike was silent; he stood there looking at the images of his little girl, art work that a doctor might hang in his home. He watched her heart beat, her chest rise and fall. He was humbled at technology; and he was grateful she still was alive. Everyone stood silently looking at each other.

 Mike broke the silence.
"Doctor Sims, Hodgins...I trust you with my life, I know you are only doing what is best for Amanda. Please, if you know she is

going to die at any point... please let us tell her that we love her and good-bye."

Doctor Sims was at a loss for words; his eyes filled with tears. His heart remembered that he never got tell his daughter goodbye; he never even got to hold her hand one last time. He looked at Mike with tears in his eyes and nodded his head.

The Project Had Begun

Stefan went back to the cabin, got on the internet and ordered the finest sculpting tools out of Italy that money could buy. Now all he had to do was wait, wait for them to arrive. All artists, including architects never go anywhere without a drawing pad. It could be 3:00 in the morning; it could be midnight; it could be in the middle of the day, but always an idea pops into his head, and if you do not draw it, you may never see it again.

He remembered that in the back of his SUV, behind the back seat, was his portfolio with the drawing pads. Once back inside cabin he drew the basic shapes of the rock that looked like Amanda and then he continued through the body, making the exact shirt that she wore on the last trip, drawing the smile on her face, the pants that formed her legs, one boot and one leg. He sketched her smiling. Even though the event was tragic, he wanted people to remember the smile he saw.

He would have had no problem being an artist. Several of the top art schools in the country had offered Stefan full scholarships, but he wanted to build buildings. He did not want to go to art school. He wanted the challenge of making something stand for a lifetime. Sculpting was like building a building, it took creative thought and precise workmanship. There was no jury to judge his work, there was only the memories of Amanda to compare to. When he was finished with the piece, he started to cry. Like a photograph, Amanda was standing at Eagle's Nest, just like she did that last day. For the first time in a long time, he was not angry at God. For the first time in a long time, he was not angry at life. For the first time in a long time, his only thoughts were of how much he loved her, how beautiful she was, how much she made his heart beat—how happy she made him in that short time. He didn't think about the tragedy. He didn't think about her voice echoing into the darkness. He thought about the smile and the happy times. Now that he had the drawing all that was left was waiting for the tools to arrive. He was excited, though his *project* had changed the end result would be a powerful statement.

Waiting to Start

Stefan still had a couple of days before the tools arrived. He slept for the first time, got up the next morning, and found himself doing little things around the house to occupy his time. Don't misunderstand, there was not an hour that went by that Stefan did not have tears in his eyes. She was his life. He sat at the table, got out another sheet of paper; he started drawing him and Amanda together with his head down, her head lying against his chest and his hands across her back. The side of her breast was exposed, and her naked bottom was leaning against the wall. When he was done, he remembered the way she felt in his arms. Though naked, how pure it was, how innocent, and he thought to himself, "If I can find two rocks close together that I could make this sculpture out of, then people would not only see her, but would also see us in our purest form, like Adam and Eve."

He put the pencil down and went out to the balcony. He had not eaten in several days and went to the fridge, and there were some tomatoes, carrots, and some lettuce left over. He took a knife and just cut it into chunks - he did not bother to make it pretty – threw it in a bowl and walked out to the balcony and sat down. There was nothing in his life that did not remind him of Amanda. There was nothing that he cared to think about. The Boston project was a memory. It meant nothing to him anymore. His family had not even crossed his mind in days.

He looked on the counter in the kitchen. The letter to his
mother was still there. He did not remove it. He left it. He did
not intend to cancel his leap of love. The leap of love was still
part of what had now become a driving ambition. Stefan loved
challenges. He loved to make things happen when other
people said they could not and what he was going to do with
the sculptures had nothing to do with money, success, fame,
but it had everything to do with the love that he had for
Amanda. He figured the two sculptures would take him a week
each to do, and he could wait two weeks because every time
that he drove the hammer, deep in his heart and soul he
would be whispering to Amanda, telling her that soon he
would be with her.

He could not sleep. He woke up reaching for Amanda, and she
was not there. He cried out to God in anger, maybe more out
of agony than anger. He broke down in tears. He got out of bed
and went into the kitchen. The cabin was quiet with a
mountain chill in the air. As he sat down at the table he saw
his drawing pad. Stefan found himself doing another drawing
around midnight. He started drawing Amanda sleeping in bed
with the silk against her skin, the perfect shape of her body.
Her left breast was exposed, her hair down to the side of her
face, softly lying against the pillow. He made the drawing as
innocent and intimate as it was the night he watched her

sleep. Again, he thought if people could see this, they would stay in bed with their lovers longer. They would let them sleep and see their beauty. How could he not do this as a tribute to Amanda?

The tools had arrived, and Stefan felt actual excitement—not a joyful excitement, not in anticipation of having a marvelous time, but a responsibility, like a carpenter who buys a hammer or a saw. They're excited, or they are happy to have the right tools; because they know with the tools they can accomplish what it is that they are trying to do.

Geneses

Stefan was excited about working on the sculpture. He headed out about 6pm. Stefan finally reached the South side of the property. He parked his car at the edge of the woods and started his hike. He was a full mile from the park; he did not want to draw attention to his vehicle. He got G.P.S. locations when he was walking the park during the day. He knew exactly where the rocks were that he wanted to sculpt by his G.P.S. location. This mountain was a granite mountain, so it was a mountain that accepted sculpting. He read up on everything about how to handle the different materials, what tools to use, how much pressure, what angles, and what the best hours were to work. Stefan was a perfectionist, so understanding a craft was the first step in doing anything. He got to the rock that looked like Amanda, a life size boulder shaped like the outline of her body, and he started working. Tears fell down his eyes; it was as if he was digging in sand, desperate to free her. He worked and worked, hours passed. In the distance, you could hear the chisel—you could hear the hammer striking the metal rods. It was much like the sound of the men working on the railroad. Men working in the mountains, the echo of hammers driving spikes over and over. As the sun began to rise, Stefan realized he was exhausted. He stepped back and looked at Amanda. It was her. He walked over and put his hand on her face. He could hear her voice talking to him. The sculpture was almost complete, just minor sanding and smoothing of some rough edges; yet, he had duplicated her to such a strong degree that he felt the need to touch her. It was not about an artist bragging on the quality of his work; it was about a man who loved so deeply that even out of stone it moved him to see her. He did not go back to the truck. He lay down beside her and fell asleep with tears in his eyes.

He was startled at the sound of a leaf blower. A park ranger was walking towards him clearing the trail of leaves. Stefan grabbed his backpack and disappeared as fast as he could, moving into the thick woods. He worried if he were caught, then everything would be ruined. He waited there in the thick brush until he knew that he could mingle among the tourists. He knew it would not be too long because the large chains of the front gate were sliding across the metal, like being dragged on the ground, they made an obvious sound. People started walking by, but it did not take long for a crowd to gather at the sculpture of Amanda. Stefan knew park rangers soon would be coming so he quickly made his way through the crowd, headed up the mountain, and into the woods. He knew it was a close call; he would have to leave earlier next time. He made his way home. He was tired and exhausted. It was 10:30am; he made his way to the guest bedroom and laid down on the bed. He did not even bother to take of the dirty clothes or pull the sheets back. He was simply worn out. Stefan had the alarm set for 4pm in the afternoon. This would give him time to awake, get a shower, and grab something to eat before heading to Eagle's Nest.   Stefan was sore, but he felt happy about the work he had done the previous night. He looked forward to returning to the mountain. He took a quick shower and grabbed something to eat. He parked in the same spot as he had the night before and headed through the woods to the mountain. He arrived as the sun began to set. He stayed in the woods about 200 feet away from the sculpture waiting for complete darkness to come. He heard the chain pull across the large gates as they closed. He knew the tourists had gone home, but he still was worried about park rangers catching him. Before he stepped out of the bushes, he heard two people approaching. Two park rangers walked over to the sculpture of Amanda. They stood there talking about how much it looked like her. They questioned who and when someone could have done the work. One of the rangers spoke up,

"Did you know that today we broke the attendance record, the one that was set the first day the park was opened to the public? I know it is because of the death of Amanda that people are coming to visit the park." The other ranger nodded her head.

 "Wow, this looks like her; last year she was giving a speech at the auditorium... it really looks like her."

"I wonder if we hired someone to do the sculpture. I never have seen so many tourists."

The two rangers stood there for a long time talking about all the things that Amanda had done for the park. They kept saying over and over how the sculpture resembled Amanda.

An hour passed, and the two rangers had gone home. Stefan walked up to Amanda; he noticed that the dew around her hair had run down the sides of her face...it looked like she was crying. He walked over and wiped the tears off her eyes. He worked through the night and finished up the detail work. He saw the tops of the trees begin to glow orange. He knew that the sun soon would follow. It was time to head home. He walked fifty feet backwards and stood there looking at her. He put his hand across his mouth and chin and studied the details. Stefan wanted her to be perfect. He wanted anyone that saw her see exactly what Amanda looked like, not like in a photograph. He wanted them to be able to walk around and just see how incredibly beautiful this woman was. He was a perfectionist if she made his heart beat then he knew that he had accomplished a true representation of her. Because part of her was projecting from the mountain, he was only able to walk around two sides, but all the proportions were correct, the angles were correct. It was as if Amanda was standing in front of him; it looked just like Amanda.

Stefan took his tools and headed home, but not until after he walked over and held her hand and told her how much he missed her. He went back to the cabin. He grabbed food on the way home only to keep himself fit until the project was complete. Using a fifteen pound hammer and chisels was hard on anyone of strength, but Stefan had not eaten well in over two months, so he knew that he had to eat healthy foods. He had to prepare his body to be able to do the rigorous work. He was on a mission to be with Amanda. He felt this was like going to college and she was going to wait home for him to return. He knew that this would take a little time, but there was no changing the fact that he had planned on stepping off where she had died, giving his life in the same tragic way. He felt obligated or driven to leave in the same manner that she lost her life.

Stefan sharpened his tools and laid down to go to bed. It was not long until the nightmares started again, but this time it seemed worse. This time, instead of the rain blocking out his vision of her face he could see her face clearly. He could hear her begging for her life.

"Please, Stefan. I love you. Don't you love me?
Don't you love me, Stefan?
Don't let me go."

He started crying out her name, yelling her name in his sleep. He woke up. He looked to the left, and he looked to the right... He was alone. He started sobbing out of control. Though he did everything possible to save Amanda, he still felt he could have held on tighter. He was tormented by her voice. He got up and took a shower in the guest bathroom. Even there, being naked in the cabin reminded him of Amanda's body. The warmth of her breasts and the soft lips. He leaned against the tile and closed his eyes. Often, sexual contact is forgotten after losing someone. The longing to hear their voice seems to replace the desire to be intimate. Stefan thought of Amanda standing in the water as the steam rose off her wet body, the round breasts and curves that made his heart race.

"I Love you Stefan; I love you more than you will ever know. I am waiting." Amanda turned around and walked away, slowly disappearing into the steam of the shower.

"Amanda!" Stefan cried out her name in hopes she would stop. She was gone; he opened his eyes, looked around the shower, and he realized he was alone.

Quiet Thoughts

Betty was in shock. Amanda's condition was improving; how in the world could she be getting worse now? She trusted the doctors, she knew that they were only doing what was best for Amanda. In all her years as a parent, even with Michael being Autistic, no doctor had ever been so frank with her. It made her cry, but it also made her trust them more. She sat by Amanda's bed day after day with little change. She was constantly praying to God to help her understand or at least accept whatever was ahead of them. Julie told her that it would be 5 days this time. Then, if everything goes well, they would bring the body temperature back to normal and see what happens. How does a mother not speak to her dying child for five days? Even though the doctors did not like Betty holding Amanda's hand they allowed it because they knew that she needed something to look forward to each day. Anything that gave her hope was a welcomed thing. Amanda was struggling against the pain in her head. Betty imagined falling and hitting her own head against the concrete, how much that would hurt. Amanda bounced against rocks for over twenty feet before wedging between two rocks. She was a beautiful woman, but the accident was going to leave scars that would never go away. The right side of her face got the most damage. Like a glass was broken into little pieces, and then dragged across the side of her face, the skin peeled up, and the muscles were damaged. None of that mattered because she still was breathing, fighting to stay on this side of Heaven. Betty looked around the room, there were no cards or anything from the outside world. As far as the world was concerned, Amanda Wilson was dead. No one knew that she was alive. Betty told people at the church Mike and she were at a retreat for families that had lost a child. Even Michael was invited on the weekends. She asked the church to pray for the family, just pray that everyone would be healed. Though it seemed strange to many people, the family requested Amanda's burial to be a private one. They gave a date to the media and told them that the family refused any type of donation, stating it was the wish of Amanda that no one give financially for her death. The media ran with that, as well. Christian woman dies and tells people to spend money on their own families before charities. It was not what the Wilson's said but at least it kept the media from following them.   Because Michael was autistic, the helicopter rides could be explained as different trips for testing.   It all was taxing...Betty wanted to tell the truth. What she desperately wanted was for Amanda to get better.

What People Are Saying

Stefan arrived at Eagle's Nest to continue the sculpture. He got his gear and put it in a backpack and headed towards the mountain.   There was a group of tourists standing there looking at the sculpture of Amanda. Stefan stepped into the woods, into the shadows so no one could see him, and he watched them. He wanted to see what their reaction was and try to hear what they were saying.

He heard one lady say to another, "I bet that is, yes that is the girl that died. God, she's beautiful."

Stefan started to cry.

He heard the compassion in their voices and, no matter if it was an old man or a young girl, the story made the heart ache. People were talking about how beautiful Amanda was.   One lady spoke up and said,

  "What a tragedy. She was such a beautiful woman. What a terrible, terrible thing to have happened."

Stefan felt accomplished for the first time in a long time. He felt that what he'd accomplished was exactly what he had set out to do. He started to walk over, but then he realized it would become about him, and people would be asking him questions. Even though he wanted to tell them about Amanda, he knew that it if he revealed himself it would turn personal. Then the attention would be on him instead of Amanda. He didn't care about his story or even his life because soon he was going to go be with Amanda. They didn't know the whole story. He felt it was important for the world to understand and get to know Amanda.   This was the reason Stefan did the sculpture, not fame or attention but to honor the woman he loved.   A man willing to die for a woman clearly loved her. No one could deny that he loved her.

The next day, right at sunset—he got up and got his gear and headed back. He parked his car in the woods a mile away from the entrance and walked through the trees to the mountain. He placed little reflectors on the trees so he could find his way in and out in the dark. They were the size of a pea. They were like spider eyes when a little light touched them. They reflect light, so that way with just a small flashlight he could turn it off and on and keep his path straight in and out of the woods without drawing attention.

It was still light. He wanted to get to the mountain before dark. That way he could find the next form in the rocks that would match the sculpture that he was doing. This sculpture was of Amanda and him together naked.   200 feet up the path was the perfect formation of rock that would lend itself to him to start his work. Through the night, the chisel clanged against the spike, like a railroad being built in the darkness. The hammer fell against the metal and the mountains echoed the tingling sound.

Stefan worked with a candle. He didn't want a powerful light that would expose him to the world. It was obvious that someone was working on the mountain. Stefan was deliberate. He was diligent. He'd work through the night until he started seeing the sky turn orange, and it was like taking a flashlight and finding a lost jewel. He packed his chiseling tools, he stepped back and looked at the figure. As the light started to rise, the details of his work became visible, you could see the sculpture that he had created. This was a complex work; this particular piece could not possibly have been done by just any sculptor. The details were perfect and the body exact, so much so you almost blushed standing next to it.

He had finished with just the outer figure which was Amanda's body and his arms coming around. The rest of his head and shoulders were still rock, it looked as if the mountain was holding her instead of a man. By the time he got back to the house, it was around 9:00 in the morning. He was exhausted and fell asleep. He had been working on a piece that was passion, intimacy between him and Amanda. And, so, he dreamed about her. He dreamed about making love to her, looking into her eyes and feeling her heart beat, about how he held her tight as she shook, her lips trembled. He saw that look of sheer exhaustion from the body releasing passion, the tears in her eyes when he whispered that he loved her. Right now all he had was his dreams with her. The reality was that he was alone.

He slept through the day and woke up mid afternoon. He went into the kitchen to make himself something to eat. He sat at the table and began to eat salmon. He remembered how

Amanda talked about how she liked salmon. He still followed a healthy diet. Some people, knowing that they only would be around for a few more weeks, might eat anything and everything that was unhealthy for them. Really, what would it matter? He easily could see where they might eat cake, ice cream and junk food, but it wasn't who he was. He was a person that did things the way they're supposed to be done. Some people would argue that suicide was giving up on life; it was the cowardly way out of regret. Stefan felt that his choice to commit suicide, to him, wasn't an act of giving up on life, but it was an act of love. It was an act of wanting to be with someone that was his soul mate. He didn't want to live if she were not on this earth. He wanted to die the same way she'd died... to prove how much he loved her.

He headed to the mountain again before dark, and as he approached there were more people, ten times the amount as the night before.

National Attention

There was a man taking pictures with a flash camera. He wasn't an ordinary photographer. You could tell. He had a bag full of extra equipment, and he wore a badge, some kind of ID tag. Stefan had not been to town. The only time he went to town was to get groceries. This wasn't a lifestyle change, meaning he wasn't planning on being around for months. He'd just bought enough groceries, water and wine to last him for a few weeks. He did not realize that his sculptures were starting to draw attention. He had turned his phone off because he didn't want to talk to the outside world. His family was concerned. No one knew where he was.

He watched as people gather around the sculptures and talked. Every time it was always the same thing. They would talk about the beautiful woman, and the tragedy.   How dangerous climbing mountains was, how terrible losing the love of your life would be.

They said, "You know the guy she was in love with was the guy that built The Falls. He was an architect. He disappeared when she died, he got so distraught that he gave up on life, and no one knows where he's at."

He shook his head and made his way further up the mountain through the woods so people wouldn't see him. He came to his next sculpture. Even though it was half finished, there were about twenty people standing around; a news reporter and a camera man. Stefan squatted down behind the bushes so no one would see him. He heard the reporter telling his story, telling the world about the tragedy of a beautiful woman. No one knew who was doing the sculptures, was it Stefan Rogers? He was known as a great artist and no one has seen him since the accident. This work clearly wasn't done by an amateur but somebody with precision.

The news media had picked up the story, and it had become national news. The state and the forestry division would not allow access after-hours because of insurances and the circus that it would cause for people to come in after hours. The main gates were locked at dark.

After everyone had left, Stefan sat there with tears in his eyes. He looked across from him and the woman that he loved was naked, lying against the rocks in a position that he had felt in his arms. He went to work. The chisels reshaped the rough rock. Like sand on the skin, they were knocked away until there was a smooth surface. He finished his body with his head tilted down, and it was like an intimate photograph. Standing from the perfect angle, the side of her breast and part of her nipple were exposed, pressed against his chest. Every detail was perfect, just like the work he did on buildings. Stefan was a perfectionist. He wasn't going to do anything that wasn't incredible.

He laid his head against the side of her face and told her, "Soon. I will see you soon."

Foot Steps

Stefan had fallen asleep before morning came. He was exhausted. He had laid against the tree by the trail, and before he realized it his eyes had closed. His tools were all in a bag in the bushes behind him. He suddenly awoke to the sound of footsteps in the leaves. It wasn't a dream. It was a park ranger. It was an older woman with stripes on her arms, clearly she was an officer of some kind. Stefan was worried that he was going to go to jail—or worse—he would not be allowed to return to the mountain.   She stood there without a smile on her face.

"What is your name?" she asked in a stern voice.

 "Stefan," He replied.

 "Stefan, do you realize that the park has not opened yet and that you're on federal land trespassing?"

He knew he was in trouble, and he said,

"Yeah."

He did not know what else to say, he told her,

"I just wanted to see the sculptures."

Tears filled his eyes because he was afraid that he wasn't going to be able to return.

The officer walked over to the sculpture and said,

"It's amazing, isn't it?"

"Yeah, it is." Stefan replied.

"You know, you look an awful lot like the guy that's holding that woman."

Tears rolled down his face as he listened to her.

"Stefan, I met you and Amanda the day you went for your hike. You bought the passes from me. Amanda was an extraordinary woman."

Stefan just stared at the lady with his eyes full of tears and said, "Yeah, she was."

The woman told Stefan that she had been sent by the forest division to find out who was doing the work. She arrived earlier in the night to find out how the sculptures were being made and who was responsible. It doesn't take a rocket scientist to know that the work being done takes hours. The forestry division knew that it was attracting a lot of attention, which meant a lot of dollars to help pay the offset of taking care of the national wildlife, so they didn't want the sculptures to stop. They weren't interested in prosecuting someone. They were as curious as anybody else as to who was doing them and why. So they sent Mrs. Johnson to investigate who was doing the work.

"Stefan, I've been watching you all night from over there. I know you're hurting. I heard you crying. I saw you touch her face. We're not going to tell anyone. In fact, we've decided that we're going to fence in the outer perimeter of the mountain so no one can get on the property—to protect the work that you're doing. We want you to know that we feel it was a terrible, terrible tragedy and what you've done is only out of respect and love for a woman. There's not enough of that in this world."

Stefan couldn't believe what he was hearing. The tears rolled down his face as she was talking. He only could think of Amanda, and what a compliment to her that the forestry division knew of her; and they respected her so much they were willing for the rock faces to be turned into sculptures in her honor, but more so that a man trespassing would not be prosecuted but allowed to continue.

Mrs. Johnson said, "Stefan, we're going to put a lock on your point of entry. We're going to make that a gate, and I'm going to give you the key. No one else is going to have the key. You can come and go as you will. They're okay with you continuing to do sculptures, but you have to promise us that you won't do anything to disappoint us and give the forestry division a bad name because Amanda loved this mountain. All of us that knew her, loved her. Not as much as you did Stefan, but we did." She reached her arms out and held Stefan as he started to shake. It seemed unclear if he were distraught over hiding from the world, hiding from life, hiding from the pain, or if it was his exhaustion, but he wept in her arms.

As the sun rose Mrs. Johnson told him,

"The gates are fixing to be opened. You need to go ahead and make your way home, so people don't see you. And you need to shave your head or let it grow long, grow a beard, do something because your picture is all over the media. No one knows where you've gone. Contact your parents and let them know you're okay. Everyone's worried about you Stefan. You don't have to go home, but at least let the people that love you know you're okay."

Stefan was overwhelmed. No one had ever showed him that much compassion before. The forestry division, which is normally pretty stringent on their rules and regulations, was now allowing a man to come on the property, deface a national forest, carve the rocks, and make sculptures because he loved a woman so much that he wanted the world to see her. Stefan did not tell the forest ranger what his plans were because he did not want her to know. He knew that if he told her that he planned on jumping off, then they would have kept him from coming on the property all together.   He was grateful for everything that they were doing for him and Amanda. He made his way through the woods, back to his car. There was a long line of traffic. People were already lined up to go to Eagle's Nest and see the work of Stefan. He was a mile from the entrance and yet cars went around the bend. He knew that taking his car could lead to issues if he got pulled over or someone recognized his tag or car. He decided that from now on he would have to bike to the park and be more careful.

Once he got back to the cabin he did what he had been doing for the last couple of weeks. He walked into the kitchen and sat at the table and started drawing. This time he wanted to draw whom she was, so he drew her kneeling down and planting a tree. This was something that Amanda would have done and had done on many occasions, something that was not about intimacy was not about him, but it was about her. So… people would understand that she believed in a cause. He drew a deer lying next to her, a fawn, watching while she planted the tree. He thought to himself if people could see this side of Amanda then they would truly understand the depth of the person that he had loved. They truly would understand what a loss for the world her death was. He fell asleep at the table—something he had not done in years.

Silent Night

Stefan completed the sculpture of Amanda lying down. It was moving. He tried to make all the pieces to scale as much as possible, life-like, as though you could walk up and touch the side of her face and feel as though you were touching her. There wasn't anything exposed that shouldn't have been. He was respectful, but he also wanted to make sure that the world saw her as the beautiful specimen that she was—a creature crafted by God himself in the perfect image of a woman.

As he made his way at sunrise, he decided that instead of walking through the forest to get to his bicycle, he would go out the main trail. As he made his way down the mountain, he came to the first crowd of people. They were admiring the sculpture of Amanda and Stefan in an intimate pose. There were more than fifteen people taking pictures. He felt a little awkward, as though they were part of his private moment. Then he heard people talking about how beautiful Amanda was, how intimate the positions of the body, how much in love they looked. Tears filled his eyes as he realized total strangers could see what he and Amanda felt together, carved in stone.

He looked like a bum, or what the world would call a bum—a homeless person. His clothes were barely hanging onto his body. He had a beard and long hair. He wore a baseball cap and sunglasses. Further down the trail he walked, and he came upon the entrance, the start of the mountain climb. And that is the sculpture of Amanda smiling.

There were more than fifty people standing there. Women, children, and elderly men would walk up and put their arms around the sculpture of Amanda as relatives and friends would take pictures. As Stefan stood there and listened, it was as if a record was being replayed. Over and over people would tell the story and like all stories and all tales the truth seemed to be stretched and the events more heroic or dramatic than the story before. Imagine being in love. Imagine not just being in love, but to be infatuated to a point where every time you breathe you think of them. That's how it was for Stefan. He loved Amanda more than he loved life. They had grown close in a short period of time. Their hearts beat the same. There wasn't a night when he fell asleep that he did not think about her, long to touch her, and now, after the tragedy, he stood among fifty people listening to their stories about her. One of the downsides of working on the sculptures and being around the people as he leaves is that he hears the story of her tragedy every day. Not that he doesn't hear it in his mind and soul, not that he's not reminded every day inside his heart.

Metal and Flesh

Skilled craftsmen make mistakes. The bad thing is when working with your hands and metal if an accident happens...it can change your life. Stefan was not a full time sculptor though he was beyond average. In fact, it certainly could be concluded that he was one of the best in the country. He was still capable of a terrible accident. He was doing some final work on the sculpture of Amanda kneeling. It was a tight fit up against the side of the mountain. Stefan's body was twisted, he was tired, and he could not get the strike angle, but he was determined to finish before leaving. Unsure if he slipped or he just lost control of the heavy tools, his hammer glazed the right side of the chisel causing all of the weight and force of the hammer to impact his right hand. You could hear the bones shatter like little egg shells smashed against a table. The blood soaked into the rock. Stefan almost passed out from the pain. He took his shirt off and wrapped the hand. The skin was split, and at least two fingers were broken. He struggled to get home; for the first time he feared that he would not complete the project.

Stefan made his way home. He was exhausted emotionally, mentally, and physically. His hands bled from the slipped chisel. He was left handed, so the hand that constantly gets the abuse is his right hand—swollen, bruised, and his skin split. He ran cold water on it. It was numb. Stefan knew now that his project was coming to an end that he had one more sculpture to do: the final sculpture. He had planned this to be the final sculpture, but when he did his investigation to find the rocks that were shaped well enough to be able to do the work, he found they were lower down the mountain than he hoped. He decided he needed to do one final sculpture after that. There would be five altogether, and the final sculpture would be at the spot where she slipped off. The one before was only 100 feet lower. It was to be her kneeling down, planting a pine tree. Stefan figured that as he made the sculpture kneeling to the ground, he would actually plant a small tree between her hands and the tree would grow. To the right there would be a deer, a fawn. Amanda loved wildlife. She loved the wilderness—all of the animals. What better tribute than to do a sculpture of her with nature showing how much she loved the outdoors?

The final piece was the only one in question. He sat down at the table. He hadn't slept or ate yet, but he sat down to sketch his final drawing. He considered just a hand reaching out—empty, though people knew the events of the accident, he felt that was too dramatic. So, he decided the final piece would be the two of them embraced, fully clothed, in a passionate kiss, so when people reached that point of the mountain and they looked out over the valley hundreds of feet below, they would know that on that spot, love once stood. He loved her so much that he was willing to perish the same way she did, to leave his life with the same means hers ended.

The final sculpture would be an embrace and kiss. His project now had a deadline. There were no more sculptures; when he finished these last two, it would be over, and all he would have to do is wait for the rain. The time he thought was only going to be a couple days now had turned into weeks. He didn't waver from his thought, from the goal of his project. Sadly, Stefan had no idea Amanda was still alive.

Amanda in His Dreams

He thought of Amanda. He dreamed of her hands on his chest, but tonight was different.   Stefan was making love to Amanda, her skin warm and her eyes soft. They kissed as if it were their first time making love. Stefan's heart was pounding, he could not separate his dream from reality—it all seemed terribly real. He could taste her lips, feel her body hot beneath his. He stopped to tell her he loved her. Amanda reached up and put her finger on his lips.

"Shh... Stefan, why are you crying?"

"I had this terrible dream that you and I were hiking, and you died... I could not save you!"

Stefan rolled over, and Amanda got on top of him and listened as he went on to tell about the last few weeks.

"It felt so real, I had gone and lived with my parents, and the world said we were like Romeo and Juliet. I carved all these sculptures of you, in fact, I crushed my hand..."

As he was describing the damage to his hand he put his right hand out in front of her, and it was busted, bruised and swollen.   Stefan got quiet, he looked at Amanda and said with tears in his eyes,

"You aren't real are you?"

She was quiet...

"Amanda I cannot go on living this life without you. There is no meaning. Every day I miss you, there is an emptiness inside that I cannot fill; I want to die."

Amanda laid her head on his chest and told him,

"Stefan, you don't have to do that, I'm always with you. All you have to do is close your eyes. I'm always with you, I am always with you...." Amanda slowly disappeared into the darkness.

Stefan started sobbing. He sat up, Amanda was gone. It was only 4:00 in the afternoon. He had only slept for five hours. He went into the bathroom and stood in front of the mirror. He didn't recognize the man he saw. He had a beard and long hair. He could see the bones in his cheeks. He could see how lonely he was. People have a look of despair when they lose a loved one. It's a sadness that never seems to go away. Even though it had been months since Amanda's death, Stefan looked as if it was yesterday. He looked like someone had just called him with the news and he was reliving it.

Stefan knew the next two sculptures were the most complex. In order to finish before the rainy season, he was going to have to work faster. He took three pain pills. His hands—blistered and bruised were the tools that carried out his mission. He loaded his backpack, took some bananas and protein bars, and headed out the door. Once he got to the gate hidden in the woods he parked his bike in the bushes where no one could find it. Then he got his gear and walked the mile through the woods to the mountain. Tonight he wanted to get a sense of what people saw and felt when they came from the base of the mountain. He made his way through the thick forest to the front of the trail. The first sculpture was Amanda smiling. It was not unusual for fifty to a hundred people to be standing around looking at the sculpture and talking about the story. The forestry division posted a plaque in honor of Amanda which listed all of her incredible contributions to the forestry division. It was a beautiful plaque. Amanda would have been proud. He stood there and looked at the sculpture of her. He desperately wanted to go over and touch her face, but there were too many people standing around, he didn't want to draw attention.

He made his way up the trail, but it wasn't like the original hike where there was freedom to walk at a pace you felt like it. Now there were so many people that you had to wait in line. As he made his way up the trail, he came to the next sculpture, an embrace of passion. Amanda, half naked, lying in his arms—in his embrace. This sculpture got a different response from the crowd. They talked about how in love the young couple looked, her beautiful body, and how lucky he was to have had the incredible experience. Stefan wasn't the only one crying. It seemed that women were especially moved by the story. Seeing the embrace brought the reality of the loss of love. Stefan made his way further up the mountain, as he came around the bend, to the left was the sculpture of Amanda sleeping. This seemed to have a different impact on the crowd. At this point, people weren't talking as much about the couple, but they seemed to reflect on the sadness of the event, how beautiful she was, and how tragic for such a beautiful woman to have lost her life—the young man must be in torment.

Stefan pushed his way through the crowd, reached out, and put his hand on her shoulder as tears melted into his beard. He whispered,

"Soon. Soon."

The Calm Before the Storm

Julie could see Betty was not doing well. She called Mike and told him that when he arrived in town to have Betty get ready in the morning like she was going to the hospital. Julie would swing by the hotel and pick her and Michael up as a surprise. The sun rose slowly above the edge of the city. Michael was already awake and playing on his games. Mike told Betty she needed to get ready, he was going to go to the office to check on their employee. It was code for "the Hospital and Amanda" so Michael would not catch on.

"Betty you need to spend some time with Michael and get your mind off of the office. I was not supposed to tell you, but Julie is stopping by. She has plans for you and Michael." Betty smiled; it was almost all as if everything was okay, like this was a weekend trip for fun. Mike gave her a kiss goodbye and told her that he loved her. He went to Michael and asked him,

"Who is the greatest?"

"I am the greatest," Michael said with a smile.

The door was not closed for more than five minutes and Julie was knocking. Julie was tired, she had worked a 10 hour shift ending only 6 hours ago. She knew Betty needed a break.

"You ready to go? Let's go, we are going to have a blast."

"Julie you are so wonderful..."

"You don't know where we are going yet. Come on Michael let's get going.

You want to ride a train?"

Michael's eyes got big and he repeated "Julie

ride train." It was not a question but an answer to the question. Like taking the only important thing out of the question and telling the person you agree.

Julie had a picture of the train they were going to ride. It was an old steam engine, something out of the old west. Michael's eyes grew big and he grinned from ear to ear. "Train, ride train."

They climbed into Julie's car. Michael put his ear plugs in to listen to music. The ride to the train station was about an hour. Julie and Betty did not talk much, but for Betty it was like going to the Bahamas. It was a break, a moment to let her worries be held by the nurses, doctors and Mike. For a few hours, her world would be free of pain and fear... as much as possible.

They had a great time. Michael loved the open cars and the cool mountain breeze flowing through his hair. He had nothing on his mind but the sound of the tracks, the steam rising into the air and the giant wheels that went round and round. It was late afternoon by the time they got back to the hotel. Michael went and sat down on the couch and started playing video games.

"Julie, thank you so much for what you have done for my family. I know you are doing everything you possibly can for

Amanda. I hope one day you will get a chance to talk to her."

"Hey… She is going to make it, she is a fighter. God is on your side. I honestly do not know how you stay so strong. You are an amazing woman. You and Mike are an example of your faith, a reason for people to believe."

They hugged each other like sisters. Betty wiped her tears and told her that she would see her at the office tomorrow.

"Tell Julie good-bye…"

"Bye Julie." Michael said after a short glance in her direction. Julie smiled and told Betty that she would see her tomorrow

Trying to Find Reason

Again, Stefan returned to the group that was heading further up the mountain. He got to the point where the rocks had a strong enough shape that he could sculpt Amanda planting the tree. He didn't stop. It was still light, so he followed the group further up the mountain. He came to the spot where Amanda had passed, where the tragedy had taken place. The forestry division had made a plaque. It was two-fold. The forestry division had placed two plaques at this point. One was marking the spot that Amanda lost her life, and the other was a sign stating the danger of the slippery rocks.

Stefan went over and sat down on a medium sized boulder and listened to the crowd talk about the story and how tragic the events were though Stefan had heard it a thousand times. But more importantly he had actually lived it. He was not immune to the emotions found in the voices of women, the sadness, and tears in the eyes of those standing nearby. He was amazed that so many people were compassionate. Though he felt guilty, he never heard anyone say that it was his fault. In fact, every time someone told the story, they were empathetic and felt immense grief—noting that Stefan did everything he could to save her.

Every once in a while, his name would be brought up in regards to what happened to him. Some people would ask, did he kill himself? No one has seen him for months.

One lady said, "I heard that 20/20 is offering 4 million dollars if he'll come forward and do an interview."

A woman responded and said,

"I believe that he's the one doing those sculptures. You know he was an artist in college. They say that he was capable of doing this work."

An older woman argued, "This isn't the work of an amateur. This is the work of a professional."

There was banter back and forth, an argument of how talented Stefan could have been.

"But love causes you to do things that you're not capable of doing. It gives you powers that you don't realize," a short woman said, standing next to the edge.

Stefan was overwhelmed by the magnitude of the conversations—his life had turned into a story. He left the crowd and headed further up the mountain where only a few people had gone.   The top of Eagle's Nest was no longer the attraction. Though many people still went there, the bulk of visitors came to Eagle's Nest for the tragedy and to see the sculptures, so not everyone went to the top, only a select few. Stefan made his way towards the top of the mountain. For him, this was an emotional climb. It was the first time that he returned to the top of the mountain. Though, in the final project, his plan was to follow the path that Amanda and he had climbed, this was the first time that he had decided to walk to the top.

Stefan made his way up the top of the mountain. The view was incredible. There were only eight other people walking around. He felt alone. He felt Amanda, though he was alone. He remembered holding her and kissing her.

When most people stand at the edge of Heaven reflect on their life, how wonderful it was, how beautiful. But for Stefan the edge of Heaven meant that he was close to Amanda, yet he couldn't see her, couldn't touch her.

He looked around and as far as he could see there wasn't a cloud. The sky was blue. He got angry, not at Amanda directly, but at the fact that he had not been aware of the danger. Why couldn't the state have posted signs about the rocks being slippery before they ever climbed? He would have questioned her about it. It always seems, policies always seem to change after tragedy strikes. This certainly was no different. Unfortunately, he was part of the tragedy.

How could God let such evil happen, such destruction? That would be the first thought of anyone that God is to blame. Though Stefan was angry, he wasn't angry at God. He never felt the things terrible in life were God's doing. He wasn't blind to the fact that Amanda's death had brought thousands of dollars to the national forestry division, had brought attention to the environment. There wasn't a newscast in the last couple of months that didn't mention the ecology. Debates were now being talked about on subjects that were silent until the death of an environmentalist. It seemed that her death was the catalyst for much of society to open their eyes about the impact man had on his environment.

Stefan noticed a mountain ridge off to the right and a cascading waterfall. Honestly it was the first time he had thought about the falls and the project that Amanda and he were working on. It was the first time that the past came into his mind, a life that most would have loved to live - a life that Stefan walked away from. For you see he replaced one project with another, but his new project would be his last. In his mind, it was the perfect ending to a career of anticipation.

A Story Told

Stefan wanted the story Amanda to live on long after his death. After hearing all the conversation of the tourist at the sculptures, Stefan was afraid that his suicide would be just that, a story about a nut that committed suicide. That was not the story nor was it what he wanted people to remember about him, but more importantly he did not want his actions to take away from the story of Amanda. He decided the only way to accomplish the facts to be made public after his death was to have his story professionally written. In passing through the store in town, he heard a reporter on the news named Melissa Morrison. She was a well-known and talented reporter. She had spent time in Afghanistan as well as other harsh environments putting herself at risk so that facts would be known. Stefan felt she was the best qualified to handle the situation. He had no intent on her knowing all the facts, but he knew that after his passing she would be able to explain why he chose to leave this earth.   He contacted the news station and asked to speak to Melissa. By chance, Melissa was at the station that morning for her weekly meeting with the editor.

"Hello, this is Melissa Morrison, how can I help you?"

"Melissa, this is Stefan Rogers... I would like to meet you in private."

Melissa felt a tingle, this was the hottest ticket on the news. Everyone was searching for this guy. Was it even him?

"I am a very busy person and do not have time to chase

pranks."

"Melissa, you spent 6 months in Afghanistan, graduated from Berkeley with a 3.9 GPA and your entire family members are psychologists. I do not have a lot of time to try and convince you. So here is information that no other person would have taken the time to find out about me but you. I read your book, I know that you are a driven reporter and have already done your background check on me. My father was a POW and yes, I have a watch made from the shackles he brought back."

Melissa realized she was truly talking to Stefan Rogers.

"Okay Stefan I believe you. Why me? You have half the country trying to write your story, why me?"

"The precise reason you are asking... Everyone else would have been counting money or planning on retiring off the interview, but you want facts. Melissa this is not an interview but a book deal only. It comes with very strict conditions. I trust you but I need to know you will follow my wishes. If you agree you will have the story of your career, the exclusive story. Are you interested?"

Melissa barely could speak, not once did she think of money, but the story, just as Stefan said. Amanda's tragedy was the hottest story out there and no one could crack it because the only person alive to tell it was Stefan Rogers—the ghost.

"Absolutely Stefan, I want the story!"

"Meet me at Momma's Place about an hour South of Eagle's Nest, tomorrow at 3pm. Not a word to anyone, see you tomorrow." And then Stefan hung up.

Melissa Yelled "YES" everyone in her office looked at her puzzled. She had promised Stefan that the meeting would stay between them. She told the other people in the office that she just confirmed her flight to Europe for vacation next month. Nobody believed her because she was not an actress. Her boss asked her to come into his office for a minute before she left.

"What was that all about out there?"
"You know I can't tell you! Brad, just leave it alone. Trust me on this one, I need to go off the radar for a few weeks."

"Okay Melissa, you're the best I have got...the only one that is allowed *not* answer my questions. What do you need?"

Melissa had worked for Brad for over ten years the stations ratings have increased every year mainly because of Melissa's insight and professional approach to the investigative reporting.

"I need to be off the radar for a few weeks, maybe a month. I cannot tell you who, but the fish is on. Honestly, I am not sure what we are going to get out of it, but it will be the biggest story this station has ever covered. I promise I will stay in touch. Oh I need a rental car and five thousand in cash, this one has to be off the grid—no trace."

Melissa, was the best in the industry. She knew her value and what it cost to get the job done right. She was a woman of her word. If she took the company car it could be traced, a credit card and a G.P.S. posed similar problems; if anyone caught wind she was near Eagle's Nest then it could compromise her promise to Stefan.

"Okay see Joan, I want receipts this time, and I am not kidding!" Brad told her as she was walking out his door.

A Bond is Formed

How often does a woman get to interview a person that is considered Romeo? Stories circulated by the rescue paramedics and hospital personnel that heard Stefan crying out for Amanda. It was Hollywood. *Tragedy strikes couple in love, woman lost and man cries out her name*. Even though she was a reporter, Melissa was still a woman beneath the business suit and the tough questions. She was a passionate person that learned to hide or protect her feelings. This meeting was one that not only professionally she was looking forward to but as a woman she was interested in meeting a man that loved so deeply he would cry out her name.

She arrived at the restaurant at a quarter till 3. She did not want to be too early but felt the fact Stefan was an architect he most likely would expect her to be on time. She walked into the lobby, a little over dressed for the meeting but still not in a business suit. She was smart enough to know a restaurant called "Mama's Place," most likely did not have a strict dress code.   Stefan saw her walk in he was sitting at the table, the one he felt belong to him and Amanda. There was no denying Melissa, she was 5'6'' with olive skin and brown hair. She had a professional look, some women have a smile that make men notice, and others carry themselves with such class a smile is only extra— men notice. The waitress walked up to Melissa, and said.

"Stefan is already sitting over there waiting for you."
Melissa looked in the direction where the waitress was
pointing, but Stefan was not there, or at least the Stefan from
the photographs. She looked at the man in an old plaid shirt,
sunglasses and hair that clearly was unkempt. The most
striking thing about the man in the direction of the window
was his hands were rough. The right hand was wrapped in a
bandage. Melissa was a top investigative report. She had
already surmised that Stefan was doing the sculptures, so
when she saw the damaged hand she knew that was Stefan.
As she walked up to the table, Stefan stood up and pulled the
seat out for her and told her hello.

"Melissa, I am Stefan. I uh—I am glad you came. I am sorry... I
have not talked to anyone in a long time."

"Hi Stefan, thank you for inviting me." Melissa looked at his
hand, she noticed it needed medical attention. Her time in
Afghanistan gave her some insight into tissue damage.
Stefan saw her looking at it, he moved it off the table and
placed it in his lap. Melissa did not say a word. Over the years,
she had learned to listen first then speak. Especially in the case
of a person that was in hiding, the last thing you want to do is
say the wrong thing and cause them to change their mind
about telling you their story. Stefan was not used to talking to

people. Even when things were going well, he was not the person in the room to strike up a conversation. He did not mind, but he was not a social person, he liked keeping to himself.

"Stefan, tell me about Amanda; how did you meet?"

Stefan stirred his coffee slowly. "I was in the planning stages of a project with Boston to construct another building downtown. Amanda and I met in the elevator in the falls building. We were on or way to a meeting together. She made me forget about being scared of heights, she made me forget about a lot of things. She was just incredible, the most remarkable woman I had ever met." Stefan was relaxing, he put the damaged hand on the other side of his coffee cup all most as if to keep his hands warm. Stefan told her all about the environmental things Amanda had done. The lectures and awareness campaigns, so many things that made him fall in love with her. He talked about her faith and love for the wilderness.

"Melissa when I looked at her I shook inside... Does that make sense? I loved her so much I wanted to be around her all the time. She made me feel like a kid again. I believed in fairy tales, the writing of Shakespeare, Penofpoet and Wilcox, for once I understand the passion that they spoke of. My life finally made sense."

"She sounds like she was truly dedicated, passionate... I think you are right she was a very special woman. Stefan few people find their soul mates, the person God made for them, I think Amanda was yours."

He looked up at Melissa because as with Amanda, another woman his age was talking about God. In the last five years, very few people his age talked about God. Most of the people he was around were self-absorbed and invincible. They did not feel the need to believe in fables or give credit to the logic of a creator.

"Let me tell you why you are here, what it is that I want from you. Amanda meant the world to me, I loved her more than life and still do. Now that she is gone I need to do whatever I can; tell the world about how incredible she was and help her dreams still come true. She had a younger brother named Michael. He is Autistic, she loved him more than anything. Her eyes would light up every time she talked about him."
Stefan had tears in his eyes, he had to stop for a minute and take a deep breath. Thinking of Amanda was not as emotionally hard as talking about her, sharing your heart and soul about a woman you loved and watched die.

"Michael needs to be taken care of financially. Amanda's parents, well like our parents are getting older, Amanda was the safety net for Michael. The plan was for him to live with her if something happened to their mom and dad. You see what I mean? She had the whole world, but she was willing to give her life for her little brother." Melissa saw Stefan's pain, the tears in his eyes, the way he was tormented by her death. She normally did not get emotional, she was a reporter, a person that gathered facts. She was a professional; interviews were just part of the job. Letting yourself get emotional was distracting and could cause you to miss out on important information but in this case she felt tears running down the sides of her face. Every sentence made her want to write his story, Amanda's story, a professional woman that was driven, not by money but love. The love for her Brother, the environment and Stefan. Melissa knew that this would end up a movie, Hollywood desperately looks for a tragedy that ends with passion. This was a story that needed to be told.

"Stefan how long ago did you hit your hand?" Stefan looked at her, he started to make up a lie, but he knew that she had figured out that he was doing the sculptures. "Not too long ago."

"I think it is broken. Stefan you need to get it looked at."

"I can't, people will find out it is me that is doing the sculptures and that would change everything that I have planned."

"What do you mean, 'planned'?"

"Listen, we are getting sidetracked. All I want you to do is write the story. I will tell you everything about our relationship and the project, but you cannot go public until I tell you. Can you make that promise?"

"That is fine, Stefan, I understand. What is *the project*?"

"I call the sculptures the project, just like all the buildings that I have worked on. It is just a name that is easy to refer to."

"How many sculptures are you planning?"

"There are 5 all together, I have completed 3."

"I need to go with you when you are working on them."

"I don't think so..."

"Stefan you want me to do the job right? Then you need to allow me to spend the rest of the project with you. I have to understand your passion and the way you think, to be able to fully appreciate your love for Amanda."

Stefan knew that Melissa was driven. If he did not agree she most likely would not do the book,

"Okay that is fine, but I work alone, and you are going to get dirty..."

Melissa laughed, "My time in Afghanistan probably taught me how to deal with getting a little dirty. Stefan about your hand, we need to..."

Stefan cut her off, "Listen I am not going to the doctor, don't bring it up again, I only need it to hold the chisel. I have to go; this is where I am staying. I will call you in a couple days."

Melissa reached across the table and put her hand on Stefan's arm,

"Everything is going to be fine, thank you for giving me a chance to write your story Stefan. We will tell the world about how wonderful Amanda was and the incredible gift of the project that you have done for her. I am honored to be given this chance." She smiled and looked deep into his eyes. The sadness was haunting, the last time she saw it was when a soldier died in her arms, while his wounded comrade kept telling her, "Do something... please you got to do something!" A look of loss, the loss of love. Love does not have to be sexual, but it is an energy that cannot be stopped; it's a connection that causes the heart to beat and tears to fall. Stefan loved Amanda then and now.

Melissa Thinks about Stefan

The conversation with Stefan was a bit overwhelming for Melissa. She had never experienced a man talk more passionately about a woman than Stefan spoke of Amanda. Sure, she had read Shakespeare and Penofpoet; stories that to her were inspiration for young women to search out the right man. But she had never heard such deep love and compassion coming out of the voice of a man. There was an air of sincerity, an aura of compassion. As they left, she actually felt alone, she thought to herself if Amanda shared that same energy with Stefan, what would it have been like for Amanda to be away from him. For the first time, in a long time Melissa actually thought about feelings. As a reporter, you are taught to keep the story at a distance from your heart. You set it aside like it's not real, a play or a good book you are reading. You're not connected, it's just something that you're reporting. But Stefan's story connected with Melissa. It connected on an emotional level and her spiritual level. The very part of a woman that causes the heart to beat. So this was an experience for Melissa that she had not had before. Most of her stories were factual and to the point and sometimes controversial, but this was a story about love in its purest form, a tragedy that you can't even imagine the amount of suffering.

Reflections

Stefan went back to Eagle's Nest. There was no time to waste. If anything the conversation with Melissa made him want the project over sooner. He wanted to be with Amanda, he wanted to stop hurting inside. As he walked through the crowd of people looking at the sculptures he was amazed at what they were saying. Stefan was moved by the stories he heard even though he was a main character in a tragedy written for life and not the screen or the stage. Stefan still understood compassion and understood how powerful the story was. He knew that Amanda's death had opened up dialogue about the environment. Because of whom she was society became aware of the loss of an advocate, someone that would stand up and fight to protect the wilderness and wildlife. Stefan was proud of her. He desperately wished that she could have been on this earth longer. He realized every day the impact that she had on everyone around her. Ultimately that's what bothered him. It wasn't that a life ends, but the question—why someone so remarkable would not be given a chance to live a long life? He thought of the drug dealers, the pimps, and the businessmen that were as crooked as a ninety degree angle. Why would they be given the chance to live long and healthy lives? A life of destruction, a life destroying all beauty. He couldn't understand it. He started to walk up the mountain and he noticed a young couple coming towards him, holding hands. And he broke down. He remembered how warm she felt against him, how the sound of her voice echoed in his ear. He thought about the way she felt when she slept in his arms. Amanda was more than an infatuation. She was more than a girl that he liked. Amanda was Stefan's soul mate, when she perished, a part of him died. The only way he felt that he ever would feel whole again was if he went to be with her.

He made his way up the mountain, making as little eye contact as possible, and avoiding the stares. He avoided conversation. He kept his head down like an alcoholic or an addict. He made his way through the crowd, down the mountain, and into the woods. There was an area that was lower than the trail that no one could see. He had spent so much time down in the gulley that the ground around the boulder had an indentation where he sat. He would sit there and reflect on Amanda, reflect on his mission. He got to his spot and sat down. The leaves were colorful. The wind blew just enough to hear the leaves rustling in the trees above. Stefan knew that the true rainy season was only weeks if not days away. The storm that had come through the day of the tragedy was a fluke. It didn't show up on any radar, on any newscast that they had been watching, but soon the mountain region would fall into the bad weather, the rainy season, where you have afternoon and evening showers. That was the time that Stefan would return to Amanda's side. That was the time that his project would be over. So he knew that he only had a week, maybe two before he had to be finished. He looked at his hand. His pinky finger and ring finger on the right side were twisted. He had missed the chisel and struck them directly against the rock, breaking some bones. He feared going to the hospital because they may have put two and two together and put a stop to the sculpting. So he iced it every night until the swelling went down enough so he could hold the chisel again. He had scars, though the scars on his hand were visible, the scar to his heart had not healed. His hand was swollen. Like arthritis, he could barely close it, but he was determined to finish the project. Like all his projects before, Stefan was not a man that missed a deadline.

As night time began to fall and the last of the tourists left the mountain he could hear the giant gate being closed and the chains being pulled through, like a prisoner walking along death row. Stefan got his backpack and made his way up the mountain. He got to the point where the new sculpture would begin. He sat down, and for the first time he wondered if he was doing the right thing. He wondered if this was about Amanda or was it about his grief and trying to deal with it. He wondered if ending his life would only bring attention to him instead of her. I wouldn't say that he was confused. What I would say is that he was engulfed in the tragedy that had been two months ago. His project lasted longer than he expected. Though there had been a few rainy days that could have ended the project; just like all of his previous buildings, the change orders for add-ons simply extend the time of the project. His final project had changed. The original concept was to go to the mountain and leave this earth the same way she did, but because of the change orders, alterations, the time frame had to be adjusted to get all the change orders completed in time for the final ending.

Stefan wiped the tears from his eyes and went over to the rocks and started working. Just like the evenings before, the sound of the chisels rang throughout the mountain air. The sculptor once again was sculpting.

Melissa knew that Stefan was doing the work. She sat in front of her TV and watched the news as they broadcast photographs of the different sculptures found at Eagle's Nest. She was an investigative reporter. The old saying, "Don't leave any rock unturned," she followed that to a T.

She removed the photographs that she had taken of each sculpture and laid them on the table.

She made a map of the mountain and marked where each sculpture had been done. She noticed a pattern. Not only a pattern about Amanda, a reflection of their relationship, but she noticed that Stefan was working his way up the mountain. What she didn't understand or yet was to comprehend was why. What was Stefan doing? Why was he working his way up the mountain?

Melissa poured a glass of wine and sat at her living room table. She put on some Yo-Yo Ma and listened as the cello broke the silence. She got out her laptop and replayed the recordings of the interview with Stefan. She started writing the story that one day would change her life.

Melissa was worried for Stefan. After interviewing him and listening to his heart and soul, she knew that he had died inside—the tragedy was something that was so overwhelming that his system shut down. She looked at the placement of the sculptures, what each scene meant. As an investigative reporter, she was taught to read between the lines and it seemed that like building the ground floor of a skyscraper, Stefan was building a building and at some point the building would have to stop. At some point, there would be a ceiling and what did that mean? The first floor was the lobby, the grandeur of the building, and that was the first sculpture, a sculpture of Amanda smiling. Then the next floor, it was an intimate sculpture of him and her together, showing the world how much they loved each other; the next floor, Amanda sleeping, tranquility. Her by herself taking away the attention from Stefan and putting it back on her because of his deep affection for her.

The Sculpture became more about Amanda than their love story. Stefan seemed to be fading out of the picture. Melissa didn't know how many more sculptures, but she looked at the mountain and realized that where Amanda fell was only another 300 feet up the mountain; it seemed he was doing work 150 to 200 feet in between sculptures. Was he going to do work all the way to the top? Was he just going to do sculptures up to where she fell? And what if and why would he stop? Melissa looked at each sculpture and tried to think what it was that Stefan was trying to say. And then she felt a chill up her spine, "Don't do it." She had figured out the ending to his project. She figured out what he was planning, or she thought so. The only way to find out was to confront Stefan.

No Change in Amanda

Amanda's body temperature had gone back down. Though it was a step in the right direction there was a long ways to go. Imagine climbing Mount Everest. It was like that, climbing Mount Everest without knowing how to climb. Amanda was in the best Hospital she could possibly be in, the best equipment available to help her but it was up to her to want to live. Betty knew by the facial expressions of Julie and the rest of the nurses that things were better but that was not enough. There was a hidden worry, a look of concern.

Doctor Hodgins came into the room and asked Betty if she had a minute to talk. Like all the times before Betty knew that this was not a good conversation but one that was sure to cause more worry.

"Betty, I know I asked you not to mention your son or Stefan to Amanda. However, I believe now that it may be the only way to get her back. She is in a coma that we have not caused. Her system is reluctant to hit the re start button if you will. Talk to her about anything and everything that is important. Let her know you and your husband are here and love her. Michael and Stefan reached her last time, lets pray she still is listening. Tell her that you love her and need her to open her eyes. We are running out of time we need her to be able to communicate to find out how extensive the damage to her brain may be."

Betty looked at Doctor Hodgins, His eyes showed how worried he was.   She knew from reading medical journals that the longer Amanda stayed in a coma the less of a chance she had to live a normal life...if she ever woke up.

"When?   Mike gets off at three today, he is flying up with Jim and Michael tonight. Can we do it in the morning? "

"Yes, tomorrow morning will be fine. Get some sleep tonight, call the church and get them praying for the family."

Betty gave doctor Hodgins a long hug. She walked back in Amanda's room and held her hand while the nurses continued to check equipment and change bandages.

Release of Pain

Stefan continued to chisel into the night. It seemed that he had picked up the pace, there was an urgency to the work. The world was getting to Know about Amanda because of his sculptures. His work had drawn more attention to the environment than he possibly could have hoped for. The forestry division was receiving thousands of dollars in donations. The environment was getting national attention for her causes. Stefan couldn't be more pleased, but he still was concerned about making his deadline. The project was coming to an end.

The sky changing from black to orange was an indicator that the day was close at hand, and soon he would need to head home. Stefan was exhausted. He had worked faster than any other night before. He was three quarters done with her body. She was kneeling on the ground with outstretched hands. He planted a small tree between them. There wasn't a sculpture that wasn't passionate, accurate of her description. Everything that he did, he did out of the memory of her. Imagine your favorite dessert. Imagine it was done in stone, so precise that it made your mouth water. These are the emotions that Stefan got as he finished the sculptures of Amanda. In a way, they were bringing her back to him. From a rough rock came the soft skin of the woman he loved.

He packed his backpack up and started walking through the woods heading back to his bicycle. For some reason, today seemed more agonizing than the rest. He was tired. He was tired of the night shift, of sleeping in the heart of the day. The only conversation that he had was with Melissa, a reporter. When Stefan got to the house, he did the normal routine of icing his hand and sitting down on the couch. He didn't question the project. It never was a question. Like all the buildings, once he started one he became obsessed with its completion. He devoted all his energy and time to the project to make sure it was completed on schedule. He had no interest in changing his course, he was going to see it through.

Melissa Lays the Cards Down

He drifted off to sleep from sheer exhaustion. He was thinking about Amanda, the first dinner that they shared, the sparkle in her eye as the sun set, he was awoken by a knock on the door. At first he didn't know what the noise was, then he realized it was the front door. He got up and walked to the window and looked out. He saw Melissa's car in the driveway, and for a moment he thought of ignoring it, pretending that he wasn't home like she was a kid selling candy or Jehovah witnesses. She knocked again, this time harder. Stefan figured if he was going to get any sleep at all he should let her in, see what she wants, and then send her on her way. He opened the door. Melissa was standing there with a smile. She had a bag in her hand and a cup of coffee.

"Stefan, I figured that I'd bring you breakfast."

He looked at her and smiled. It wasn't on purpose, it simply was a reaction. How does one not smile when someone drives fifty miles out of her way to bring breakfast?

"Well are you going to let me in or... am I supposed to leave it on the porch?"

He laughed and apologized and opened the screen door and said, "Come on in. The house is a mess, but come on in."

Stefan had left the drawings of the sculptures table. Melissa came in and sat down with the bag of doughnuts and coffee at the table, she noticed the drawings. She didn't say a word.

As Stefan walked towards the guest room he told her, "Give me a minute. Let me go get cleaned up."

She said, "That's fine."

Stefan went into the bedroom. He knew he smelled. He got a quick shower and brushed his teeth, put on some jogging pants, and an old T-shirt. Stefan had a thing about his toes. He didn't like women to see his toes, so he put on a pair of socks and walked back into the living room where Melissa was sitting at the table holding the pictures - the drawings of the sculptures. She looked at Stefan, She got up and walked over and reached for his right hand, it was swollen. It was black and blue with cuts from where the hammer had broken the skin. She turned his hands over, and there were several broken blisters. Tears filled her eyes. He could see her worry, the realization of sacrifice he was making not to win favor, but to express his love for Amanda. They just moved together like a magnet, drawn together by a force out of their control. Stefan slowly closed his arms around her and started to cry. For a long moment, they silently held each other.

Stefan finally was releasing some of the pain that he had held inside. He was in the arms of a woman. It wasn't Amanda. It wasn't his mother, but it was a caring soul that felt deeper than the surface. Melissa put both of her hands on each side of his beard and kissed him on the forehead.

"Stefan, let's sit down for a minute and talk. I need to talk to you."

He followed her over to the couch. Stefan sat down facing her and she sat on the other side almost Indian style, with one leg hanging over the edge. She put her hand against the side of her face and leaned to the back of the couch.

"Talk to me, Stefan. Tell me what's going on. Tell me about this project that you're working on."

Tears streamed down his face. The drops resting on his beard like dew on leaves. Stefan looked at the ground and then he glanced up at her.

"It's something I've got to do for Amanda."

"Stefan, you've got to be honest with me. I'm a reporter. I know there's always more to a story than what people think. What is this project you keep talking about? What is it, Stefan?"

The tears seemed to increase. Like a lie detector, the closer to the truth the more tears fell.

Stefan looked at Melissa, "I couldn't save her. I had her in my hands, and I couldn't save her."

Melissa reached over and put her hand on his arm, "Stefan, it's not your fault. It's a terrible, terrible thing, but it's not your fault. It's an accident. It was just an accident, Stefan."

Stefan didn't respond. He looked at Melissa, his eyes red from crying and then he looked towards the mountain.

"Stefan, I've seen the sculptures that you've done, and I understand you're telling a story. I've seen the drawings of the work that you're working on and the one that has not been started. Is that all of them? Are you going to continue up the mountain? How does this project end, Stefan? You want me to write your story, but you have to be honest with me and tell me what story I am writing."

Melissa found herself getting upset.

She found her voice cracking and then she blurted it out, "Am I writing the death of Amanda—the tragedy, or am I writing the death of the architect? Is that your plan, to give up, to kill yourself?"

Stefan looked out to the mountain as the tears dripped off his beard. Wiping them away did no good because as soon as he wiped them away more came.

"You don't understand. You don't understand," he said in a shaking voice. "You weren't there."

"Please, Stefan. Make me understand. Make me understand why someone so talented would give up everything for a cause? For a woman that is already gone. There are so many people that love you, Stefan. You could do so well in this world. You've brought so much attention to the causes that Amanda believed in. Why would you give it all up? What do you think it's going to change?"

Stefan was silent. He looked at Melissa, "It's not going to

change anything, Melissa. I died the second her hand slipped out of mine. I wake up every day only preparing myself to complete this project. All I think about is being with Amanda. I have no feelings. I have no concerns of what this world is or what it will become. I loved her more than life. I couldn't save her."

Melissa got up. She was frustrated. There was something about Stefan that tugged at her heart. Maybe it was his compassion. Maybe it was his love for Amanda, but there was something there... he'd become more than a story. She found herself thinking about him during the day and now she knew, she knew what her fear had been telling her that Stefan was planning on ending his life.

She paced back and forth, "How are you getting away with doing these sculptures? Why hasn't the forestry division stopped you? Do they know your plan? Do they know you're planning on killing yourself?"

Stefan said in a low voice, "I knew I should have never talked to you. I knew I should have never told you anything about what I was doing."

"Stefan, I'm a reporter. There are certain things in life that are based on facts. You can't be on government property unless they allow you. The forestry division could have stopped you a long time ago.   There's got to be a reason why they're allowing you to build these sculptures."

She got emotional, "And I know they wouldn't be letting you do this if they knew you were going to kill yourself... They wouldn't."

She was crying. Stefan stood up and put his arms around her, "Stop Melissa. You've got to stop. Please don't cry. You've got to stop. Please stop."

Melissa put her arms around him and held him tight, she laid her head on his shoulder and cried. Stefan rubbed his hand on her back and then as they started to separate, her cheek went across his beard, and she paused in front of his face, lips inches apart. Stefan's heartbeat was racing. Melissa kissed him, a passionate kiss. It wasn't sexual. It wasn't lustful. It was passionate. She put both hands on each side of his beard and held his face in her hands and kissed him deeply. With tears in her eyes she put her hands on his shoulders and pushed off as they both were shocked at the event.

Melissa said, "I'm so sorry, Stefan. I shouldn't have done that. I'm so, so sorry."

Stefan shook his head, "It's okay. It's okay. It was me too. It's okay."

Melissa walked over to the window and looked out as Stefan stood there trying to figure out what just happened.

"Stefan, I'll write your story. As a reporter, I'm bound to tell the truth, but please reconsider the outcome. There are people that care about you deeply. Please think about them."

Stefan went over and he looked her in the eyes, "I've got to finish my project. I started it. I've got to finish it."

Again, Melissa started to cry. "Change your project, Stefan. Do an amendment, a change order. It doesn't have to end that way, Stefan. You still can honor Amanda. You can still make an incredible story. It doesn't have to end in your death."

Stefan looked out the window as she was talking. He looked at where the sun was, and he knew that for him to stay on schedule, he would need to go to sleep soon.

He turned to Melissa and told her, "I really appreciate the breakfast, and I hope you honor me and don't say a word of this to anyone. I've given you full rights to my story – something that may make you famous, but more importantly I trust you. I trust you to let me live life as I see fit. I need to get some sleep."

Melissa said, "Okay, I understand, but Stefan do this for me. I have one condition."

Stefan was used to board meetings that at the last second conditions were brought up and many times projects were canceled because of conditions, things were delayed.

"What condition are you asking for?"

"That you let me go with you. Let me be there when you're working on these last two pieces. Let me understand what it is that you feel. If you want me to tell your story, I need to be able to feel your story. I need to be able to understand why it is that you want to die."

Stefan thought about it for a long while. Melissa stared at him, but he didn't respond right away.

He was thinking to himself, "If I don't agree to this, she will hound me. She will possibly make it where I can't complete the project."

And he finally told her, "I will agree, Melissa, for you to accompany me at night working on the sculptures under one condition."

"Anything, Stefan. Anything."

"That in no way do you tell anyone about the end of the project, and in no way do you try to stop me from its completion."

Melissa agreed, even though stopping him from his completion was something that she desperately wanted to do. She knew that if she was reluctant to say yes he would not allow her to be by his side. So she told him that the reason for her to be there was to provide an accurate record of the events leading up to the end of the project; it was her only way of being able to write it so people would understand his logic and feelings. She gave him a deep hug and asked him what time she needed to be back.

He said, "I'm usually ready to go at 5:00. You need to get a mountain bike. We don't take a vehicle."

She said, "No problem. I'll be back here at 5:00."

She gave him a deep hug and kissed the side of his face. She put her hands on his beard and looked him in the eye and told him, "You're a good man, Stefan. Just because the project's over doesn't mean what you offer the world should end."

Stefan replied to Melissa, "Please let me do what it is that I've set out to do, please."
With tears in her eyes she nodded up and down, "Okay. I'll see you at 5:00."
She walked out the front door. Stefan stood in the living room and watched her go. He didn't walk her to her car. This wasn't a date. As he laid down on the couch to sleep, he thought about the kiss and then he thought about Amanda. He told himself that he was just emotional and needed affection; the tragedy of the event must have gotten to him. He closed his eyes and drifted off to sleep.

I'm not sure Melissa felt that taking Stefan breakfast was going to change the course of her fear, but she did leave with a feeling that she at least had a chance to talk him out of it. She had grown fond of Stefan. She always called friends and relatives to do background research on people that she wrote about.   She was amazed at how many people loved him. It's common to have a few friends. It's even more common to have friends that are willing to stab you in the back, cut you down, and tell all your dirty secrets because they feel that it's important that they tell the truth. Stefan had no friends that carried a dagger or were jealous of his hard work and personality. Not only did he not have any friends that were willing to say negative things about him, but he lived a life that was honorable, respectful. It was full of meaning and devotion. It was true that he had not had many relationships and that he had dove into his work, but it did not mean that he was not passionate. It did not mean that he was not willing to love.

She looked at the photographs of the various buildings that he built, and all of them had a common element. They all were mesmerizing. They all were passionate. They all made you think, to ponder. Melissa like many women found herself moved, not by his looks, but the ingenious of the man. The ability to create something out of nothing.

She went home and got things together that she knew she would need for the long evenings, and then she went off to bed knowing that her plan was to spend the rest of his life by his side as long as he would let her.

It seemed like he just laid down when the alarm told him it was 4:30. Stefan had only gotten six hours sleep, but there were nights that he only got two, so six hours sleep wasn't too bad. Tonight would be different. Tonight Melissa was planning on accompanying him. It wasn't Stefan's original plan. It wasn't his ideal situation, but he knew that Melissa could blow the whistle and cause his project to be canceled. The most important thing in Stefan's life was the completion of the project.

He thought back about the kiss. He tried to analyze the logic and reason behind it. It bothered him that he would kiss another woman when he was so deeply in love with Amanda. Growing up, his uncle married a woman, a beautiful woman. They were only married for three years, there was a terrible car wreck, and she was killed. One year later, his uncle got married to another woman. To this day they're still together. For years, Stefan couldn't understand how his uncle could have loved someone so deeply and get married so quickly after her death.

He thought about Melissa and the kiss, the way she felt in his arms, the comfort he felt, and the compassion. He wondered—in life when people get married for a second or third time, is it truly love or is it to replace that emptiness inside, that pain that doesn't seem to go away? It really didn't matter. He was just rambling on in his head like he often did. He went out to the garage to the grinder and sharpened his tools. He was now ready for the night's work. As he was walking back in the house, he heard a car coming down the gravel road, it was Melissa... On the back of her car, she had a mountain bike.

Melissa was fit. She wasn't a mountaineer, wasn't a hiker like Amanda, but she attended the gym regularly. She was concerned about nutrition and her health. She got out of the car and took her bike down. She put a backpack against it and walked towards the house. Stefan wasn't looking for companionship, so it wasn't a road trip. It wasn't an excursion where they would start talking as soon as they got together. He just simply said, "Hi,"

She returned the greeting, "How are you?"

"Fine. You ready to get going?"

"Yes."

It was that simple. They knew each other. They knew why they were there. Melissa knew what the project was about, and Stefan knew that Melissa was there to record his last days. They got on their bikes and headed north. Stefan had made the trip so often that he knew where they could cut through the woods, meet up with the winding road, saving them miles of senseless travel. In fact, he had traveled the shortcuts so much that they now became bike trails. It kept him out of the eye of the public and away from the roads.

Melissa thought to herself as they were going through the woods, "What a beautiful place. How incredible this would be if this ride was for pleasure and not to complete his project."

She had dated a lot of men. She was very strong willed and never gave ground on an argument. Because she was a reporter, she always did a background check on any guy interested in taking her out. Many times canceling the relationship on the second or third date because of things she found, so to be in the company of a man that was pure at heart; honest, attractive, and compassionate was something that she had not experienced before. She felt that Stefan was above average in every category that life offered. She followed him up and down the mountain path.

Halfway he pulled over and stopped at a boulder and got off the bike. He sat down and told her this is his resting spot. He normally would rest fifteen minutes before continuing. The last thing he wanted was to be panting and out of breath when he got to the mountain.

There still was a mile hike over to the face of where he would do the work, so he wanted to be physically ready when they got there. He did not want to use up all his energy just to get there quickly. Melissa took a drink of water and asked him how long ago did he start the sculptures and when did he know about the project.

Stefan explained that the original plan for the project had changed.   Originally he was to wait until it rained, go to the mountain, the spot where she died, and step off. It was only going to take one trip to the mountain. He said the first time he returned to the mountain he was surprised by the rock formation that looked like Amanda. It was the driving force to start sculpting which changed the project.   An amendment that he had not expected.

Even though he was exhausted from working on the first sculpture, He found himself sitting down and drawing new sculptures with new meanings. One thing lead to another, and now there were five. He felt it was critical that the world see Amanda in the way that he saw her.   He wanted the world to appreciate her for the beauty that she was. Melissa was moved to hear a man talk about a woman with such reverence, such compassion and devotion.   Like when a group of women get together and dream about one husband that is attentive, caring, loving, and intimate with his wife. When the others find out, they're envious. They want what they don't have.

Melissa sat there for a moment and wished that she was Amanda, wished that she had experienced the personal intimate side of Stefan. They looked at each other for a long moment and Stefan told her,

"We need to get going. It's going to be a long night. I hope you're up for it."

Melissa turned to him and said, "I spent four months in Iraq. I think I can handle a shady mountain."

Stefan broke out in a smile. He had no idea the toughness of the woman he was with.

He said, "Let's go then."

They got back on the bikes and headed through the woods.

Close to the Heart

When Melissa was in Afghanistan, she was at a military base. Her mission was to tell the story of the struggle to keep the peace in a country that had no concept of peace. This trip was different. Even though she knew lives would be lost in Afghanistan, that Americans would die, men that she got to know, the loss of life would be random and unpredictable. She was nominated for a Pulitzer Prize for her story. This story was going to be quite different. Death still was involved but it was not only predicted, but planned—she would stay with Stefan until the project was over. Stefan had stated to her that he intended on following the project through to the end. There was not going to be an alternate ending, this incredible story would end in another tragedy, a senseless death, but this one on purpose. To try to gain favor with whom? God? Amanda? Amanda had already died. How did Stefan think that taking his own life would make her feel better?

Melissa was torn and bothered.   How was she going to get through to Stefan? She knew by the size of the sculptures and the detail pretty much how long it took him to accomplish them. The max amount of time she would have is two weeks. She had 14 days to convince Stefan to change his mind, to have an alternate ending to his project. He was a logical man, and she felt if she could come up with good enough reason for him to doubt the ending, then maybe he would consider a change, but she knew he also was strong willed and he loved Amanda more than life.

They got to the spot next to the mountain where they hid the bikes. It was a thick group of small trees close together. Stefan took the bicycles, laid them sideways on the ground, and slid them up underneath the limbs so if someone happened to be hiking nearby they would never see the bikes.

It was at 6:30, the sun was setting, and the crowds were moving off the mountain. Instead of taking Melissa to the first sculpture they went to the sculpture of Amanda sleeping. They mingled in among the crowd before walking towards the upper part of the mountain. As they stood there for a moment, Melissa had the chance to hear firsthand the stories being told. She stood there with Stefan as an older woman spoke to her twenty-four-year-old daughter. She told her that love doesn't always survive, that life sometimes happens, never take the love of a man for granted, especially if you're truly in love. Melissa's eyes filled with tears as she listened to this lady talk about the importance of always telling your partner that you love them. It was as though this tragedy was the catalyst for people to rethink how they looked at love and how they treated each other.

Melissa looked at Stefan, though he had glasses on, she could tell that it was getting to him and that it was touching his heart.

She reached over and put her hand in his and told him, "So people won't think we're strangers."

He just looked at her. It was the first time that he held the hand of a woman, for the sake of holding her hand, in a long time.

After the mom and daughter moved on, Melissa turned to Stefan and told him, "I see what you mean. I had no idea the impact of your story, what people were saying. Again, Stefan, how are you allowed to do this work without the Forestry Division having you arrested? "

Stefan tells Melissa How

"When I was working on the second sculpture, a lady from the forest division showed up. It was about the time that the media was drawing attention to the works. I had fallen asleep but was awoken by the sound of someone walking. Through the woods came an officer for the forestry division. Melissa, I thought that it was all over. Not only the sculptures, but I thought I was going to go to prison. This is federal land, and according to the law, I'm federally trespassing. I was petrified. In a way, I guess I was relieved because it had been a secret so long. Finally, someone else knew what was going on. She told me that she recognized me, she had met me the day of the accident when Amanda and I had come through the gate. She went on to say that the forestry division loved Amanda." Stefan's voice started cracking.

"That they thought the world of her, and there was no finer person than her. They actually wanted to tell me that the sculptures had such a positive impact on the mountain. Their revenue increased 300%, people were lined up to come see the work and hear the story about someone that supported wildlife in the national parks. So they had made a decision that instead of prosecuting me and stopping the work, they would allow me to continue to do the sculptures as long as I didn't do anything to tarnish the reputation of the forestry division."

Melissa was shocked. What she was hearing was in direct violation of federal law. A person defacing the government's property and yet being allowed to continue. Though it didn't seem right, she was actually impressed that they cared enough to allow him to do so. She thought to herself, how tragic this ending is going to be if he kills himself, but just like the movies and stories found in books, a tragic ending would only mean more publicity, more people coming to the park. As long as he didn't do anything that would tarnish the reputation of the forest division, though his death would be tragic, it would probably double the visitors to the park.

Stefan continued to tell her about the story.

"So they had decided the only way to keep out law enforcement and the media was to put up the ten foot chain link fences around the property because the whole backside is a cliff edge and drops off some 200 feet. The only concern they had was the woods in the shape of a moon around the mountain. They went ahead and installed the ten foot fence, and they gave me a key to a gate that was hidden in the woods on the right side. It's the only key. The forestry division doesn't even have this key. That way, if law enforcement ever caught me going in the gate for whatever reason, they could claim they knew nothing about it."

Melissa was at a loss for words. She couldn't believe that a government agency would break its own laws, not to benefit themselves, but to keep alive a story about a woman that was devoted to the national parks.

The gates were locked. They could hear the big chains being pulled across. It was time for Stefan to get busy.

Melissa asked him, "Is there anything I can do?"

"No. I need to do this part by myself. You're welcome to watch or hand me a tool if I ask, but do me a favor and don't comment – don't worry about what I'm doing. Allow me to work on this by myself because I see things that you may not be able to see and if you distract me I might create a flaw. I'm a perfectionist, and I can't live with flaws."

Melissa sat down on a boulder next to where Stefan was working. Amanda's body was three quarters finished, and he continued to chisel. She was surprised at how loud the sound of the hammer hitting the chisel was, how much it stung when the bits of rock were shattered off. She now realized why Stefan had the blisters and why the hands were bruised.

He worked through the night, not saying a word. You would think Melissa would have fallen asleep, but she was mesmerized by the man, by the devotion, the heart and soul. His project was the only thing important in his life - the one thing that he could give Amanda.

After hours of working with just the light of a small candle, the sky in the distance was starting to change colors. The darkness that surrounded them was turning into light gray with a hint of orange absorbing into the base of the horizon. Melissa was getting sleepy. She had not stayed up all hours of the night for weeks on end like Stefan… She was a normal reporter, she was in bed before one or two am.   Stefan had not slept in the dark of the night for over a month, he was like a vampire. In fact, the light of the day was starting to hurt his eyes. Melissa was fascinated with Stefan, not only was he an incredible artist, but everything that he was doing was for love, not money or fame but because he loved a woman.

Melissa looked at Stefan's body, muscles that were defined curved around his ribs. He was fit, honest, kind and genuine… he was everything a woman dreamed of finding, the very man of which dreams were made. Melissa wished that he was not taken—that there was some way to convince him that leaving this earth was not the answer to his pain. She had gotten use to the sound of steel hitting steel and the spray of bits of rock hitting her arms, but she could not get over the passion that Stefan had. Her eyes would fill with tears as Stefan stopped to touch the face of Amanda. She knew that no woman ever would take Amanda's place in his heart but why must he give up?

Melissa told Stefan,

"Take a break for a minute and sit down, here drink some water. Stefan… it is amazing what you have done. It really does look like her"

"It does…" Stefan replied as a lost word or almost in regret. I believe that it looked so much like her that it made Stefan's heart hurt more. It was finished, Amanda leaning down planting a tree. The whole world now got to see the passion for nature Amanda had. The small fawn showed her love for wildlife. A photograph of rock if you will, it was simply amazing. Melissa and Stefan stood there looking at the sculpture.

"Do you ever wonder why things happen Melissa?"

Stefan began to open up to her,

 "When I was a child, and my father had suffered as a prisoner of war, I did not understand how God could allow such a good man to suffer… I still don't get it. Melissa, Amanda did nothing but praise God, nothing but try and make this world a better place."

 Stefan reached up with his dirty hands and wiped the tears from his eyes.

Melissa was silent, how could she reply to that question? She felt the same confusion Stefan did. Here in front of her was a man that was perfect in every way; a man that deserved the love of a woman and yet that gift was taken away from him. Not just taken away but literally taken out of his hands. Now he has given up on life, the very desire to live. Melissa could not help herself she went and knelt beside Stefan and wiped his face with a clean rag soaked in cool water. She felt his sorrow, they looked at each other with passion. It was not the, throw me on the ground and make love to me type of passion... Melissa would not have minded if Stefan took her to the ground and made love to her, but instead it was the passion that people have when they feel the heart of the person they are with.

They both understood what Stefan was planning on doing. It does not mean that they both agreed with the goal. Melissa did not try to use her looks to change his mind. She was very attractive, shapely and never had a problem in getting the attention of men. Just like Amanda, Melissa was not interested in the model looking guys that had thick wallets and even bigger egos. She was intelligent and knew that those things can be taken away in a heartbeat. She was looking for devotion, love, commitment... something that most men and women today do not have or have every even been taught. Melissa sat down and leaned against Stefan's chest as the trees began to glow orange. Though he was covered in sweat, rock and dust from working on the sculpture, Stefan could not help but notice that Melissa smelled nice. Melissa's heart was beating faster... She was not trying to make a move on Stefan, she just wanted to be held by him. She knew the kiss was a mistake, but she could not help but admit she wanted to feel it again. The warmth of his chest against her breasts. The heart beating and the deep sigh that follows. Stefan wrapped his arms around her and pulled her close. Melissa looked down at Stefan's swollen hand...

"Stefan you have to go to the Doctor, it looks really bad."

Back to the Cabin

Stefan did not answer her; he knew that the bones were broken. The split skin was healing, but the internal damage was still there.   Fingers that were no longer straight and lines of red where the skin had split open from the heavy hammer seemed like rivers of red. The black and blue color and the blood hot beneath the skin clearly indicated infection.

"At least let me put ice on it when we get back to the cabin. Stefan I am worried about you."

"Don't be worried about me.
You know better than that. "

Stefan told Melissa in a way that had the answer to the future. He had no interest in fixing bones when the heart was broken. He knew that his project was almost over; he could live with the pain for another week, if not days.

"We should be heading home," Stefan said.
Melissa liked the sound of calling the cabin home. Don't kid yourself she knew that it was a metaphor for a place to rest and had no meaning outside of that.
Melissa was a study of people and the mind; she was originally

supposed to be a psychologist, a career that her whole family had chosen. She was stubborn and driven to push the boundaries of the way people looked at the world around them. Melissa felt that if she could get Stefan to talk to his Mother, maybe he would reflect on how much it would bother her. Melissa did not say much on the way back to the cabin. The mountain was beautiful in the early morning light. A silent ride except the sound of the bike tires rolling over leaves. The scurry of squirrels running across the path and the wind blowing by. Once they got to the cabin they both were exhausted. She knew that sculpting was not a simple thing but clearly had no idea of the toll it took on the body. Stefan went and took a shower in the guest bathroom, he was unable to go into the master bath because that is where he and Amanda had made love. Melissa went into the master bathroom and took a shower; she felt a little out of place. Although Amanda had passed away, she could still sense her presence because the energy of their passion was so strong. Melissa thought of Stefan, more about his pain, than his body. She finished showering and put on some cotton pants and a long sleeve shirt and went out into the living room looking for Stefan, but he was not there.   She walked down the hall towards the guest room.

Inside her heart beat, maybe secretly, she hoped he was still in the shower and would call out to her and ask her to join him. She felt nervous and excited looking for him. She went into the guest room, and noticed he had crawled into bed. She stood there looking at him as the sun tried to squeeze through the small opening of the drapes. She felt so awful for him; she knew he was hurting. She crawled into bed next to him and backed up so that her body nestled against his chest. Stefan reached around her arms and pulled her close. Her heart was pounding; the skin was warm. She could feel his warm breath on her neck as he pulled her close. The last time Stefan was in bed with a woman it was Amanda in the other room. He was not feeling Melissa's body for sexual gratification, but because he needed to feel the warmth of another person.

Melissa wanted to turn around, she wanted to sit up and pull her shirt of, let Stefan feel the warmth of her breasts with his strong hands. Her body blushed as her heart beat faster. She knew that he loved Amanda; she knew that it was a matter of days before he was going to leave... not go out of town but leave this earth. Her eyes started to fill with tears, she started to cry. Her body shook not from the touch of his hand but the touch of his heart and soul. Stefan felt her shaking. He ran his hand through her hair and whispered to her. She was crying, yet Melissa was turned on by his touch. Her body was screaming to feel his hands on her breasts, she thought of how strong he was. She slowly turned towards Stefan and found comfort in his arms. She laid her head against his chest. She didn't try to kiss him, or act on her desire to take off her clothes; instead she held him tight and whispered his name over and over. She simply crawled closer, breathing with his heart and dreaming of a different road yet to come. Stefan felt her body warm against his, felt her nipples rub against his chest. He was attracted to her, but he loved Amanda. Though Stefan thought that Amanda had died, she was not gone for him. For a moment, he closed his eyes and pulled her closer into his body. He smelled Melissa's hair but imagined Amanda naked against him. Melissa moaned she could not help it her body was crying out for Stefan. Like a person lost in the wilderness, her body screamed his name. Stefan wanted her, but wasn't it truly Amanda he wanted? He was torn with emotions, torn with sorrow. Melissa placed her hand on the side of his face, just inches from kissing him.

"I can't Melissa... I can't... God you are beautiful, but I can't."

"Stefan it is okay... I understand; I know you love her, I know. Please don't think I am trying to take advantage of you."

"No Melissa... Please do not think that, I never thought that! I – I um... just see Amanda, I can't stop seeing her. I know that is a terrible thing to say!"

"Melissa had tears in her eyes because one of the reasons she was falling in love with Stefan was that he loved so deeply. Stefan close your eyes...Let me be Amanda, make love to her Stefan, I won't say a word."

Melissa felt his pain, knew that he loved her more than life... for the first time in her life she was willing to be used. Some people would not understand how she could have said that to

Stefan. How does a woman except being touched by a man thinking and wishing it was someone else. Melissa was a particularly deep person; she understood the brain more than most. She knew that Stefan's feelings as a man were conflicted with his emotional tragedy… She wanted to be Amanda, if only as surrogate. The warm touch of a woman, the temperature of the skin. Stefan kissed her deeply, but it was too much for him. He stopped and looked at her with tears in his eyes and pulled her close to his chest as he whispered,

"Melissa, I am so sorry! You don't deserve this; you're an incredible woman. "
  Melissa knew that he was tormented by his loss of Amanda.

"It's okay Stefan. I understand; I am here… I only want you to see how brilliant you are. It was not one sided—your extraordinary feelings for Amanda. According to my research, she was happier than she had ever been. I know she would want you to continue your work; I am not trying to get you to change your mind. I am trying to say that I do not believe Amanda would want you to give up."

Melissa knew it was a dangerous conversation... Stefan had just kissed her; she had no idea how he would react.
"I just miss her so much Melissa. She made me smile, laugh, and want to awake each day just to hear her voice." There was a long pause.

"I could not save her, she was calling out my name and then she was gone. It should have been me, not her but me!"

Tears fell from Melissa's eyes. She knew Stefan was hurting. She held him with compassion but inside she actually found a reason to smile. Stefan had not responded defensively; in fact, he seemed to reflect on what she said. To Melissa, it did not matter if the reason was hidden feelings for her or if he was considering the value of life. Though her tears were still of sorrow, at least she heard in his voice for the first time the notion or thought to live.

They both fell asleep wrapped together like two teenagers who were happy just feeling the heat between.

It seemed like only an hour before the alarm clock was yelling for them to wake up. Their first night, well I mean day together, their first time sleeping in the same bed. Though neither one was naked, it was the beginning of closeness which neither understood. For Stefan, Melissa was the only person that knew about his plans and was truly the only person that had the ability to call the authorities to put an end to what many people would call madness. Melissa was torn; there was a gray ethical line that she was walking. If she acknowledges that she knew his plan to kill himself, and she did not stop him then she could be charged with assisting in a suicide, for which she could face jail time, if convicted. This was bigger than selling books or newspapers-this was about a man loving a woman so much he was willing to die for her. Stefan believed that Amanda was on the other side waiting for him. Somehow death was a doorway into the next world. Stefan felt he had no reason to stay on this side. Amanda was a casualty of the relationship, had he not agreed to hike with her, she would never have died. He knew that she was paying more attention to him than the weather; he knew that he was to blame for her losing sight of safety. A storm does not just suddenly appear; she would have noticed if she were hiking by herself, she would have paid attention to the signs. The bottom line is that Stefan felt that if he had not met her she would be alive today.

Melissa leaned over and turned off the alarm clock. She kissed Stefan on the forehead and slowly got out of bed and headed down the hall to the guest room to change clothes. Stefan laid there and watched her as she walked across the room. His hand was hurting, swollen and sore. He tried closing his fingers all the way down like a fist, they went three quarters the way but the pain stopped them from closing all the way. He thought about the guitar. How was he ever going to play it again? Then he caught himself, what did it matter he was planning on killing himself in a week or so.

They got ready in separate rooms, like married couples that can no longer stand to see each other naked, they were strangers although they had kissed. Melissa came into the room and told Stefan,

"Listen, if I am going to the mountain until you finish, the best thing for me is to stay over here instead of going home every day. I mean—clearly I will sleep in the other room, but I need to stay to be close to you and not lose any valuable time we have."

"I don't want you to stay in the other room. Please stay in my room, I don't want to be alone. I promise I will keep it just friends. I need to know that you are close. You are the only person that understands why I am doing this."

Melissa was surprised at Stefan's response.

You would think that Stefan and Melissa would not be able to cry anymore, but they both felt the burning in their eyes.

"Listen we will get through this; I will be there for you Stefan. I promise that people will understand; they will read your story and never speak of Romeo and Juliet again. Amanda will be the new Juliet, and you my friend, are Romeo—no even better than Romeo."

Melissa walked over and put her arms around him and held him tight.   Melissa went into the kitchen and got out some Salmon, lettuce and vegetables. Stefan followed behind her. He stopped in the hallway and looking at her, watching her at the sink placing the salad and vegetables in a bowl. He felt as if God wanted to remind him of Amanda, the night they made love. He looked at Melissa; she was beautiful, taking nothing from Amanda, but Melissa was a terribly attractive woman. She called out to Stefan while reaching for the bowls in front of her. She called out again as she turned around.

"Stefan– There you are." He was standing in the doorway.

"What—what are you smiling about?"

"You are beautiful." Stefan said.

"Stop… come on let's eat." Melissa said with a smile on her face. She could not help it. He openly gave her a compliment that had not followed a mistake of affection.   Melissa knew this was not exactly a victory, not a war won or even a battle it was just a simple step in the right direction. He had found a reason to smile, something that she had not seen a lot of from Stefan.   In a time of immense sorrow there was a reason to smile... There was hope.

IT Is Time

Melissa looked at Stefan's hand; it was swollen and discolored. The fingers were twisted; she could see the way it was lying on the table that it was bothering him.

"Stefan I am going to go into town. I will meet you at the mountain later. I have a Friend of mine that is a doctor. I am going to go get you antibiotics for your hand. I know that you are not worried about it, but I am. The hand looks really bad and the way you are resting it tells me it is bothering you. If you do not allow me to get you help you might lose the ability to use it anymore. How would you finish the project with only one hand?"

 Stefan knew Melissa was right. The pain was getting worse, each nIght the broken bones were shaken every time the hammer struck the chisel. Stefan could tell the skin was getting hotter.

"I should have done something sooner, I know. I just did not want anyone to find out. This project is all that I have left. Melissa I don't want to go to a doctor, I can't."

"I know Stefan, Linda will get me whatever medication you need. Let me take a picture of your hand so I can show her. Tell me what you are feeling so I can describe it to her. I will tell her you are a worker that is off the books and you got hurt carrying my equipment. I can't take you to the doctor because I would lose my job and you possibly would be deported."

Melissa went into the other room to change her clothes. She

closed the door almost, maybe subconsciously she left it open a little on purpose in hopes Stefan would see her changing or even come into the room. It made for an erotic thought. Stefan noticed her walk towards the room as he got up from the table and got a drink from the refrigerator. Walking towards the guest room, he looked in the direction of the master bedroom. The door was not all the way closed, the room was dark except the light from the bathroom shining on the bed. Stefan stood there for a moment like a young man mesmerized by the shape of a woman, hoping to see something that was a secret. Melissa was sitting on the bed facing the light of bathroom. Her hour glass figure was only broken up by the silk lines of her bra . As she stood up Stefan's heart raced, the silk sparkled on the sides of her breasts as her skin reflected the soft light. He found himself thinking about making love, he turned and walked down the hall to the guest room. Though he was walking away, his body wanted to go back, she was so beautiful. His thoughts of Melissa were replaced with the thoughts of making love to Amanda, the hands against the wall, her moans that made him tense. But she was gone, he knew that in a different time he would not have hesitated to go into Melissa's room. His body wanted Melissa, but his soul wanted Amanda.

Stefan got his stuff ready to go and walked out on the deck and leaned against the rail. What an incredible place. He thought about what it would be like live there. Sleep at night and spend the day in the warm sun. Melissa looked around but did not see him,

"Stefan," she called out like they had been together for years. Then she saw him on the deck looking out across the mountain side. For a long time, there looking at the wilderness, each with their private dreams. How different it could have been if they met before the accident, before Amanda. Melissa went over and laid her head on his shoulder. "We better get going," she looked at his hand... it was red, swollen and bruised. She knew that there was a strong chance for infection.   Melissa took out her camera and began taking more pictures of his hand from several angels.

"Don't worry Stefan... she will help us; we were like sisters growing up. She never has asked questions because she knows the line of work that I do is often in the gray."

Stefan was quiet.

"Melissa, I have to go. Do you remember how to get to the gate in the woods?"

"Yes, twenty steps north of the oak tree that looks like a giant, Y."

"Yep you're right... Be careful, I will see you soon."

It was not like he was going off to work, and she was taking the kids to school, but none the less it made her smile. He said, "I will see you soon..." indicating to her he looked forward to her company, or maybe she was just desperate for anything positive. The important thing was that he was willing to let her get the medication.

Stefan got his gear together and looked at Melissa with a smile. She followed him out the front door. She walked over and held the sides of his face and kissed his forehead. Thank you Stefan,

"I need to get going if I am going to get back tonight before it gets too dark for me to see the path... I still need and want you in my life."

Stefan waved goodbye as he got on his bike.

It's unclear if Stefan understood that Melissa was making a desperate cry for him to realize that she loved him, needed him, not just for this project but for the rest of her life. She had fallen in love with a man that was self-destructing. Her only hope was in the next few days, she would convince him to change his mind. Melissa got in her car and headed to Harperville. It was about an hour's drive to away. She couldn't help but to worry about Stefan's hand. He was such a wonderful person. Her biggest fear was that he would complete the project. The hand was just something that could cause the last few days to become more of a tragedy than it was already. She had a huge conflict in her heart. As a reporter this was the story of a lifetime. It was a frontline, behind the scenes exclusive that just did not happen in a person's career. Melissa as the human still took issue because she knew that the conclusion of his projected ended in suicide, which made her an accomplice to the act. She never really thought of an excuse or a reason to claim why she was willing to be involved. Stefan loved Amanda more than life.

When she first agreed to write the story it was based on her career and the desire to write a story she believed in. Then over time she fell in love with Stefan. Now she prayed that he would change his mind. No longer was she interested in selling books, now it was about trying to get him to realize there was a reason to live. He could love and honor Amanda the rest of his time on this earth. She knew if Amanda was alive she would want him to live. Melissa knew that many people would call her a monster, say that she let him die so she would be a famous writer, but it simply was not true. His death will be the hardest thing that she has ever experienced. In Afghanistan, during a mission that was classified; the unit she was with got pinned down. For two days, they fought, and for two days Melissa was the only person with any medical background. They ran over an IED killing the only medic they had in the unit. Melissa had two years of nursing to keep her prepared for traveling in jungles and war torn countries. When they got pinned down two of the young men were critically wounded. There were no medical supplies— lost in the explosion. Melissa did not think she just went into action. Though she did everything she possibly could, only one of the young men lived. The other one held her hand and begged her to help him even with his last breath. Melissa was not a stranger to death, but she was a stranger to seeing someone she was in love with die. Even worse how was she going to let him commit suicide in front of her? She did not even like to think of the word. Stefan and she both referred to it as the end of the project. Words like death, suicide or giving up were not spoken though they all were true descriptions of the future.

The public would want her crucified, no trial needed. The only way to understand why is to believe in love, romance. She had no plans on profiting from the book. The first meeting with Stefan she discussed that most of the money from the book would go to Stefan's family and Amanda's family with a small amount going to the forestry division. Melissa was only going to receive a basic income, a payment to make it all happen, so to speak. This was a story that was very personal for Melissa. Stefan and Melissa had become very close. Like when you read the novels of an author you become connected to the characters in the book.   The style or personality that the writer has created. Melissa was not reading a book she was up front and personal with the actual subject of the story. She not only heard his voice but felt his chest rise and fall as he breathed. Warm hands held her in the night; she was living both sides of the story. Though she had never made love to him, she could feel his passion, the intimate side that was reserved for the light of the candle and soft eyes. She was forced to understand his heart and soul; he told her of the plans that Amanda and he had.   All the memories yet made, roads traveled, and mountains climbed. Not only was she feeling Stefan's pain but she also was given a chance feel what it was like to be Amanda. To have the hands of a wonderful man pull you close when you close your eyes at night. Melissa wiped the tears from her eyes and whispered,

"You can do this Melissa—stay focused."

Melissa got in her car and headed down the driveway and turned the opposite direction away from Eagles Nest.   She was smiling; he had agreed to get help for his hand. This was a huge thing, just days earlier he did not even want to talk about it and now he was okay with trying to stop the Infection. Melissa did not say anything to Stefan because she did not want to alarm him. She had seen wounds in Afghanistan that were better looking turn into amputations. She was worried that he waited too long. Her only hope was that Linda would give her strong enough antibiotics. She prayed this would buy her the time she needed with Stefan to talk him out of finishing the project. Even though the hand was in bad shape, it still was not the biggest concern, the project had a deadline an ending that made everything else not important. Melissa's eyes started to fill with tears. She really did fall in love with him. She was angry at herself not only because she was willing to lose her career, but possibly face jail time for assisting in a suicide. She was angry that she let herself fall in love with a man that could not love her back.

Melissa wiped the tears from her eyes; she had to get a hold of herself before calling Linda. She pulled off the road under a shade tree and dialed Linda.

"Hi, how are you doing, sorry it has been a while since I called, but the reception up here is not that good?" Melissa told Linda.

"What's going Melissa, I haven't heard from you seen you left to work on that Romeo and Juliet story about the environmentalist that died?"

Linda was happy to hear from her; it had been a while. Melissa and Linda were always close growing up. Melissa had trouble talking about the project because she was so close. There was nothing that she could hide from Linda. A look in the eye or the sound of her voice and Linda knew that something was up. Linda could tell that something was bothering Melissa.

"Okay Melissa, What is wrong? You are a workaholic you have

never contacted me while on assignment. Are you ill, what's the matter?"

Melissa wanted to tell her the truth, but she knew that Linda would have an ethical responsibility to get Stefan medical help. She decided to lie to her and tell her that it was a coworker that was in trouble.

"Linda, I am in a bit of a bad situation." Melissa started to tell her the hurt worker story, but she simply could not lie to Linda.

"Listen, I am with the guy that has been doing the sculptures. Please do not ask me any questions. He has hurt his hand really badly and needs antibiotics; he cannot go to the hospital around here because the media is searching everywhere for him."

"You are with Stefan Rogers?" Linda blurted out.

"No – I mean yes, but you cannot tell anyone about this, please Linda there is more to this story than I can tell you. He is badly hurt; he needs antibiotics. I took images, so you can look at them and give me anything you can to help with the infection."

Linda did not like the conversation; she could tell there was something wrong, and Melissa was not normally evasive with her.

"What is going on, I understand not going to the hospital but why can't he have a doctor see him?"

"Linda, please, just once do not ask me questions. Please, I need to try and stop the infection in his hand. I will tell you everything when the time is right. Just for now, please trust me, I can't tell you. Please don't ask any more questions."

Melissa was hoping that Stefan would change his mind, and it would not be an issue, but she knew that if he committed suicide then an investigation of her phone records would lead to Linda. Melissa did not want Linda to know anything more than she did.

"Linda he cannot go into a pharmacy and pick up the script. Do you have the medication at your office or some at you home? What do we do?"

"I will have to go and pick it up for him. You realize that is not normal procedure. You are not involved in anything illegal, are you?"

"No– Heavens no, you know better than to ask me that. This is just a big story, and if the public finds out about his hand they will realize that he is the one doing the sculptures."

"Okay Melissa, but this is only because you are my best friend. I would not do this for anyone else; you do realize that, don't you?"

"I know; you are the greatest. I will meet you at the drug store in Harperville. Thank you so much! You are the best!"

Melissa started to cry, she was getting Stefan the medication that he needed; she only hoped that it was not too late. She was praying that the damage was not as extensive as it looked. She still had only days to try and convince him to not kill himself.

She wiped the tears just long enough to dial Stefan's Mother. She had spoken to her early on when she was trying to locate Stefan.   Melissa pulled into the parking lot of the drug store and waited for Linda. The phone rang four times before Stefan's mom picked it up.

"Mrs. Rogers?"

"Yes, who is this?"

"This is Melissa Anderson, the writer; we spoke about a month ago."

"Oh yes, I remember you. What can I help you with?"

Melissa was not sure how to respond.

"Mrs. Rogers... I am a close friend of Stefan's. Before she could say another word Stefan's mom started asking questions."

"Stefan you know where Stefan is? Is he okay? Please tell me he is okay, please I can't take not knowing."

"Mrs. Rogers Stefan is okay... I am staying with him, we are working on a project together but," Melissa paused her voice became shaky,
"Mrs. Rogers I need you to do me a favor."

"What is it dear, what is going on? Why are you getting upset?"

"I am sorry Mrs. Rogers Stefan is okay, but he is not doing well. He needs to hear from you."

Melissa had stood at the grave of children, families that had lost soldiers and not shed a tear. This was personal, she had fallen in love with Stefan. Just talking about his suffering made her cry.

Stefan's mom was getting upset. Here was a stranger telling her that her child needs to hear from her. A child that disappeared.
"Please, Melissa tell me what is going on, please."

"He is not doing well, we both know the tragedy and that he loved her so very much but he is giving up. I think if you could talk with him, talk to him like you did when he was a little boy. He thinks the world of you and I believe you are the only one that can help him."

"I will come there!"

"No, please... he is not, I mean he does not want to talk to anyone, I am the one telling you to call his phone I will get it charged and answer it. I will tell him I did not realize he did not want to talk to anyone. He needs you right now. I care for your son very much and he is hurting in a way that no one but you can help him with. Please call tomorrow at 10 am."

"Melissa thank you for being there for him, he is such a special young man. I am just heartbroken at the loss of Amanda." Her voice started to crack, "He loved her so much, just don't understand why things like this happen."

"I have to get going, I am meeting up with Stefan. I look forward to meeting you one day soon. I will get the phone turned on and charged before he gets back from town. I know he loves you very much, he needs a reason to want to get better. I am very worried about him and you are the most important thing in his life. I will call you after you guys talk and tell you what he says. He is going to be mad at me if he finds out I called you, please do not say anything. I just want him to get better. He loves you very much, Take care Mrs. Rogers."

"You too my dear, thank you so much for calling and I look forward to meeting you. Please give Stefan a hug for me, he needs to be held. You are a special woman and right now in his life he needs someone like you that understands what he has been through. I will be praying for you and him. I will call at 10 am tomorrow. Thank you again."

Stefan's mom hung up the phone and looked to the sky and said a prayer for Stefan. She wiped her tears and walked back into the living room and sat down next to the fire. She could remember her little boy so excited at Christmas time, colored paper on the floor and Sheba their little dachshund running through the paper. She wiped tears from her eyes as she looked at the clock and then her watch so that she knew when 10 am would be. Twenty four hours from now she would be talking to Stefan. A mother that loved her son more than life and a son that was fighting for the will to stay alive.

Melissa saw Linda walk towards the front door of drug store. She was still as beautiful as ever.

"Hey girl," Melissa cried out!

"Look at you...You are so beautiful! It's been almost a year, you look great. You have a glow about you, what is going on?"

Linda knew Melissa better than anyone.

"Enough with the questions," Melissa said as she hugged her tight.

Linda knew there was something wrong by the way she held

her.

"What is going on Melissa? Why are you upset?" Melissa had tears in her eyes. She desperately wanted to tell Linda, but she knew that it would put her at risk if Stefan followed through with the project as planned. "I can't talk about it Linda, please trust me I can't."

"I am here; I have always been here for you... You can tell me anything and it stays with me."

"Not this, Linda. Please, not this."
Linda started to cry because she knew her best friend was hurting, knew it was something so deep that Melissa had trouble talking.

"Well, let me see the pictures of the hand." Linda looked at each photo, enlarged them. She got quiet, she looked at Melissa.

"Melissa he needs to go to a hospital; if nothing else, let me look at it."

"No," Melissa was very quick on her response, too quick.

"What are you hiding Melissa?"
"Nothing. Please, Linda I can't talk about it."

Linda got a stern tone to her voice and said,

"You understand the trouble I will be in if this guy does not get help and they find out I dispensed him medication."

"He won't go to a hospital; he would rather die," Melissa could not help it, the tears rolled down her face because she realized what she said was the truth. The time was near that Stefan was planning on giving up or in his mind finishing the project.

"I won't ask any more questions. Give me a minute and I will go in and get the medication. I will need you to follow-up with me in a couple days and take more pictures so I can see the progress... Okay? Melissa this hand is in very bad shape. The only reason I am trusting you is because of the work you did in Afghanistan. You have learned what to be concerned with, but what is going on beneath the skin is what I am worried about."

"I know," Melissa said as she put the phone back in her pocket.

"I will be back in a few minutes..."

Melissa sat down on the curb, all she could think about was Stefan. He was such a wonderful man, how could she have possibly agreed to let him commit suicide. She thought about that moment; what would she say? How could she possibly stand there and let him do it? She knew that nothing was going to change his mind; the only chance was if she was there, she was the closest person to him other than his mother.

Linda came back out of the drug store with a large bag.

"Listen it is very important that he eats well and drinks these medicated drinks. His body is trying to fight the infection, he needs all the help he can get. He has to take two of the Vancomycin and one Hydrocodine as soon as you get to him. Ice the hand as often as you can. Do not move the hand around, because depending on the bone damage beneath the skin, it may constantly be cutting into the tissue and causing more infection. Follow the instructions about the amounts on the bottle and how often to take them."

Melissa was good with the instructions, how could she tell Linda that there was no rest for the hand. She knew that each time the hammer struck the chisel it was as if Stefan was driving another nail into his coffin not only in shortening the time before the project was over but also the possibility of a life threatening infection setting in, if it had not already done so.

"Linda thank you so much. I love you, I promise to take some pictures in a couple days. Thank you so much."

"Listen if you change your mind I will come to you. I know you care about this guy, your eyes fill with tears every time you look at the photos. I promised I would not ask any more questions, so I won't.   Just know that I love you, and I am here."

They hugged deeply, like the day Linda got married. Once again they would be heading down two different paths. Melissa was crossing ethical lines that she had never in her life considered crossing. Linda was leaving knowing in her heart and soul that Melissa was somehow in trouble. They left each other not with a smile but with tears still damp and heavy hearts.

Melissa felt good about the morning. She was getting him the help that he needed. It would be up to Stefan to change the outcome of the project. Even if he did not Melissa felt that she had done all she could to provide him with that opportunity.

The ride back to the cabin was a quiet one. The sun roof was down and the rays of light danced in and out of the car. What a beautiful day. She thought about how complex her life had been the different assignments that she had taken. Did she choose work over love? Maybe there was a Stefan out there but she never gave herself a chance to meet him. What if Stefan changed his mind? What if they did not have this terrible tragedy to live with the rest of their lives? How could she ever replace Amanda? She hit her hands on the steering wheel not out of anger at Stefan but frustration that she was in love with a man that was in love with another woman. Not just in love but he was so devoted that he was willing to die for that woman. Her eyes filled with tears again because honestly, she wanted that kind of man. She knew if Stefan gave her a chance she would love him more than Amanda, not because

Amanda did not love him but that even with him loving
Amanda, Melissa would still be by his side. She would never
ask him to let her go. Melissa was so torn. Why did she let
herself fall in love with a man that loved another woman, even
worse a man that was planning on killing himself? Again she
struck the steering wheel with her hands. She arrived at
Eagle's Nest, the park had already closed and she knew that
Stefan was working because in the distance she could hear the
sound of the hammer striking the chisel. She stood there for a
moment captured by its rhythm. Over and over he struck the
chisel slowly removing the bits of rock, closer and closer to a
finished work of art.

Stefan was on the last leg of his journey, he was on the last
sculpture. He knew that he only had a week left before the
project was to come to an end. The rainy season was
approaching, the time of year that every day the clouds would
form to the north and squeeze together and drop rain across
the mountains. The weather man was predicting the increase
chance of rain every day, ten percent, twenty percent and
even thirty percent. It seemed that the number never got
lower but continued to climb just like the birth of winter's
cold. Stefan was very dedicated, he always finished a project.
The end of this project, ironically was just that. The end.There
was not going to be two or three trips to get it right. The
sculptures were like leaving a suicide note for those left
behind. A story to explain why he left this world. The weather
was causing the days to get shorter, at least the length of time
he had daylight. He walked through the woods. He was like a
mountain lion or wolf; he moved through the shadows almost
as a ghost.   As he got his chisels out, he could hear the giant

gate close and the chains being dragged through the rings that secure it from would-be trespassers. Stefan was anxious to get started. His hand was throbbing from infection, but it had not stopped him in the past. He was devoted to accomplishing his goal. Stefan was known for finishing projects on time, he was not a quitter. Every time he worked on the sculptures it was like spending time with Amanda, he smiled inside. Each blow of the hammer caused his hand to ache, he knew that tonight he was not going to get much done. Imagine dropping a rock on your foot, pain shooting through your body like electricity that is what he felt every time the hammer hit the chisel. He was fighting pain, not fear or regret, but the pain of an infection wrapped in broken bones. The project was all that mattered to Stefan, it only meant that it would be delayed a few days. He thought about Amanda, how beautiful she was and how much he missed her. He paused for a moment and felt the side of the face of the sculpture, thinking about how soft her skin was. He missed her not just the physical touch but the conversations that were about life, the passion that caused her to awake each day trying to make a difference in this world. He loved that about her. He was consumed in making buildings. He never thought about what God had made, well, not until he met Amanda.

Amanda is Still in a Coma

Few people are grateful for the rising sun. I would say that most do not think about death or those that are less fortunate. Every morning people roll out of bed as though it is something that will never change, as though it's a given. Betty was faced with the thought that she may never hear her daughter's voice again. Each morning in the darkness she steps out of bed, a coldness fills her heart and soul like tile to bare feet. She meets Julie at the nurses' station and reviews what they are wanting her to talk to Amanda about. This time the excitement is not there, the anticipation that a response will be a step forward is not the same as when it happened the first time. Now it is function, something that must be tried to help her daughter come back. Do not miss understand me she will have tears of joy if Amanda opens her eyes or even the heart rate changes but she will not blindly hope anymore.

Sitting next to Amanda she started,

"Hey baby, I know you have been resting. We want you to know that we are all here for you. It has been too long since we have talked. I miss seeing you smile. Michael is asking for you...he misses you so much. You know his birthday is coming up in a few weeks. We want you to be there. I took Michael on a train ride yesterday, you should have seen him...he was in heaven."

Betty looked at Julie; neither one of them were smiling. Julie told her not to get discouraged, to keep talking to her about the family and things that matter to her.

"Stefan is fine, I know that he is looking forward to seeing you." The heart rate changed... Julie left the room and paged Doctors Hodgins and Sims. Betty squeezed her hand and kept talking to her. Both doctors came into the room, once again everyone was looking for her to step across the line, if you will.

"Amanda, this is Doctor Sims; can you open your eyes for me?"

"Baby open your eyes for us, I know you can hear me."

Even though Betty continued to talking to her nothing else happened. The progress of a change in heart beat meant she possibly could hear but there was not enough to cause her to step across the line from that world to this one. It was getting late and the doctors had a surgery that they were schedule for.

"Betty, can we speak in the diagnostic room for a minute?" Julie put her arm around Betty as they walked into the room.

Doctor Sims spoke up,

"Betty, we need to try find Stefan. I know your daughter loves you very much but the only response we are getting is when you talk about Michael and Stefan. Unfortunately we do not want to get Michael involved because of his condition but I feel that we should bring Stefan here and let him talk to her and hold her hand... the problem is nobody knows where he is at."

"We can go to his mother's house, I am sure she knows where he is." Julie said.

"Let's see if we can't get him here by Friday. If this does not work we will need to move her to a private facility, we have to follow the hospitals guidelines for care." Doctor Hodgins said.

Julie went to her office and called Jim from SkyVac.

"Hi Jim, I was wondering if you could help us out in the next couple days? We need to find Stefan and bring him to the hospital. Amanda is not getting any better and she still seems to be trapped inside; her heart rate increases when we talk about Stefan. We need to go to his parents' house and talk to his mother and find him. The Hospital is wanting to move her to another facility so our time is limited."

"Julie I would be able to do it Friday morning, I have all the helicopters booked until then. I will meet you on the south pad at 9 am Friday."

"Thank you Jim; you're the best."

The 9th Inning

Melissa made it to the mountain just as the sun started to set. She knew that leaving her car in the parking lot or near the front gate would attract attention. She parked about a mile from the secret entrance. She knew where the key would be and made her way through the woods to join Stefan. She had so many thoughts going through her head. She knew that this was the last one he had planned on doing. She had written down the order and amount of time it took to do the other sculptures according to Stefan and if she was lucky she had maybe a few days before the piece would be complete and the project would come to an end. There were new factors that could not be measured. How well could Stefan use the damaged hand? Did her presence slow him down, could she get him to slow down, spend a little more time talking? She was not sure but she knew that everything was coming to an end even if she did not want it to. She could see in Stefan's eyes that he wanted the project to be over. Stefan had talked about different stuff in the last few days almost like he was second guessing his decision to follow through with the project. Getting him to quit was not an option the only way that he was going to not commit suicide was to find a change order for the project, an ending that would meet all the guidelines of the original plan.   All she could hope for was that Stefan would hear what she was saying and reconsider the original plan.

The leaves crackled beneath her feet. Each step was like an elephant on china plates there was no way she could approach him without being heard. Stefan was happy to see her. She had brought a thermos with coffee and the antibiotics with her. The look in his eyes told her that he was in pain. She sat and watched him work, more than once he dropped the chisel trying to hold it in place. It was going to be a long night. The rain started to fall. Melissa knew that one thing that Stefan had to have was rain for his project to end correctly. For the last week it had rained almost every night. Melissa was reminded that time was running out.

Stefan worked through the night, Melissa was so exhausted...she had fallen asleep. By the time the sun started to rise, the body of Amanda was complete and the rough in of Stefan's body was taking shape. Stefan looked at Melissa sleeping he thought about how his life had changed. Just a month or so ago he was going through life full speed, constructing monuments of steel. Now the end had come, a lifetime of work had no meaning all he could think about was Amanda. He kissed the side of Amanda's face and told her "soon." Melissa felt a hand on her shoulder, she awoke and realized that the sun was trying to touch the sky, the world around them glowed orange. She looked at the sculpture and knew that there was not a week of time left. She could tell that there were only days, if not hours left before he was done. They did not talk much as they made their way down the mountain. Melissa helped Stefan load the bike on the back of her car. When they got to the house Stefan went off to the guest bathroom to shower. It was around 8:45 am, she plugged his cell phone in and turned it on. She laid it next to his bed on the night stand. As she was walking out of the room she noticed the bathroom door was open a little bit. She could see the glass shower door. The glass was frosted but she still could the shape of Stefan's body. She stood there and listened the water running. She found herself wishing he would call out her name. Just then the door of the shower opened and Stefan stepped towards her to reach for a towel. They both froze for a moment in time. He had no fat, he was tapered and muscular. She did not know what to say. She stuttered,

"I did not know what you wanted to eat. I – um just came in to ask you, I—sorry... so sorry." Feeling embarrassed, she rushed out of the room."

"Melissa... Wait, hold on don't worry about it. Give me a minute and I will be right there." Stefan came in the living room and sat down at the table. Melissa had fixed them a salad with salmon. Melissa was still blushing, she could not get the image of his naked body out of her mind.   They did not say much. She went to the kitchen and got a bag of ice and put it on his hand. They were both very tired. Around 9:45am they headed off to bed. Stefan laid down as Melissa laid down next to him. She placed her hand on his chest and nestled up against him like a teddy bear. Her nipples were hard against his side, his heart beat fast. She thought of trying to be physical, maybe that would change his mind. She did not want to use sex to get to him, what if he took it the wrong way and told her to leave. Her eyes started to fill with tears, then out of the darkness the phone rang. Before Stefan realized it was his phone ringing Melissa had picked it up, opened it and handed it to Stefan. There was a long pause, he was not sure what to do. Then he heard his mother's voice,

"Stefan where are you? Why have you not called me? You know how worried I get when you do not call."

There was a moment that seemed to last 2 or three minutes... "Mom, I love you Mom. I am sorry I have been just busy." Stefan's mom knew nothing about Amanda being alive and had no idea that Stefan was planning on killing himself. She was calling because she was told her son was hurting and needed to hear from her.

"Stefan, when are you coming home? Did you find the answers?"

Stefan had trouble speaking... "Mom I am doing okay, and yes I have found the answers to why I came here. I am staying in Amanda's friend's cabin. Mom, not sure I am coming home..." His eyes began to fill with tears.
"Mom I miss her so much." Melissa was watching him talk to his mother, share his heart and soul with her. She knew that there was no way she could stop Stefan from finishing his project. She felt badly for calling his mom. In a way, she felt that Stefan was now having to face his potential death and how it would hurt his mom. Then he looked at Melissa; he knew that she had charged the phone and turned it on. The look was not mean but sad. In a way, she wished he had yelled at her instead of showing his pain. His mother talked to him for about an hour. She told him all the reasons he needed to come home. How Amanda's funeral was private; no one was allowed to attend. Stefan found comfort in her voice, but he found no reason to change his project plans.

"Mom, I need to get going. I want you to know that I love you, tell Dad I love him. Mom I need to get going, really."
He hung up the phone and handed it back to Melissa. His eyes were full of tears. He reached over and pulled Melissa up against his chest and held her tight.

It was not long before they fell asleep. Just like so many days before the alarm woke them up telling that they were close to the project's end. The cycle of going to the mountain and working on the sculpture continued for two more days. Nothing had changed except the swelling in his hand had gone down. It was Thursday night, the sculpture was done. Of all the pieces, it was his finest work. Amanda and Stefan were in a kiss, her left hand was on the back of his head. The bodies tight together, an embrace of love. A final kiss goodbye or even hello. How the world would judge it he did not care. He was finished, his plans were to return Friday night.

Stefan had been following the weather and Friday night it was supposed to rain, not the small sprinkles but a solid rain. Melissa did not say a word as they got ready for bed. She never prayed harder in her life that the rain would not come. For once she hoped that the weather man was wrong. It all seemed like a dream, a crazy dream. He slept with her pulled to his body. When the afternoon came and the alarmed rang out for the last time Melissa was scared.

"Stefan please, reconsider, you have so much to give, please."

"Listen you agreed that you would not try and talk me out of it. You promised to support me in what I was doing. Melissa, I love Amanda... I am going to be with her tonight."

"Stefan I need you too, she felt vulnerable, scared and helpless."

"Melissa you can't go with me tonight. I thought I could do it with you there, but I can't. Right or wrong, I care about you, and for me this voyage has to be a happy one. How can I leave this world if I see tears in your eyes? I -um I am sorry but I am going alone tonight. Please let me go in peace. If you stop me, I will live in torment the rest of my life; please just let me go alone."

They embraced, tears fell as she whispered in his ear that she loved him, He loved her, but it was not fair because he loved Amanda. How could he stay and dream of Amanda? He was torn and broken. Stefan asked Melissa to give his mom the letter he had hand-written the first night he got to the cabin.

"Melissa tell the world that love does not die just because life is short. I loved her so much that even if I am wrong, and she is not on the other side I am willing to take that chance."

He had trouble speaking; there was a battle within him. He never thought he would meet a woman like Amanda. The tragedy left him with no hope, and an emptiness that only death could fill. Then Melissa comes along and holds him, loves him though he does not feel deserving. For a long time they held each other. Melissa was a person that felt that life was a choice of the person living. Though suicide was terrible she had seen where many people lived a hell that she felt was worse than an act of self-mercy. In the case of Stefan... she hurt as a woman. His willingness to die for Amanda made Melissa love him more.

She watched him dress in his hiking outfit. He gave her one last hug and headed out the door. She watched as he rode off towards Eagle's Nest. She sat on the steps of the cabin and cried.

Mother to Mother

The last couple days Betty did everything she could to try and reach Amanda. She talked about her childhood, the favorite things she liked to do as a child. Nothing seemed to get through to her. The only thing that seemed to change her heart rate was talking about Stefan. Betty got dressed and held Michael tight, told him how much she loved him. She kissed him on the forehead and told him that she would be home in a couple days. Mike gave his wife a hug and a sweet sad kiss as she headed out the door. They had been through so much in the last month but the real challenges seem to just be starting. They looked at each other knowing that if there was no improvement their daughter would be moved to another facility that housed people with long term conditions.

"You'll find him babe, tell his parents I am sorry we lied to them. His eyes filled with tears, I hope we have done the right thing, I hope they will understand why."
Betty met Julie in the lobby of the Hospital. They headed to the elevator pad together. They did not talk much, I believe that everyone knew how important it was to find Stefan. Jim helped the women into the helicopter. As they flew over the city heading towards the sun all Betty could do was pray.

"It looks like there is a front coming into our north late in the day. We should be fine; his parents' house is about one and a half hours west of the front."

The three did not say much as they flew across beautiful

countryside. When they approached the house Jim told Betty the governor had called the sheriff to inform the Rogers that they were coming to the house, so they would not be alarmed at the helicopter landing. As they flew over the property there were three squad cars out front of the Rogers residence.

As the helicopter touched down, Mr. and Mrs. Rogers stepped out of the back door of their home and watched as Jim and the two women walked towards the home.

Jim spoke up first with his hand stretched out to Mr. Rogers.

"Hi I am Jim Patterson with SkyVac, and this is Betty Wilson and Julie Dunaway from Saint Anthony's Hospital. We would like to talk to you about Amanda Wilson."

Betty's eyes filled with tears, Stefan's mom said... "She is alive, isn't she?"
Julie knew that this was shocking for Mr. and Mrs. Rogers...
"Can we go inside? We came here because we need your help, and I mean Stefan's help."

"Please come in, let's go into the dining room. Bob get the extra chair out of Stefan's room. Would you like some coffee? Please sit down."

Betty was having trouble talking, so Julie told the Rogers what had happened and explained who Jim was. "Mrs. Rogers,

Amanda is in a coma-like state; she is only reacting to Betty when she talks about Amanda's autistic brother or Stefan. We need Stefan to come with us and talk to Amanda. The doctors are hoping that will give her motivation to want to respond."

"Stefan is not here..."

"Do you know where he is?

He is at Eagle's Nest, I believe, I just spoke to him today. He said he was staying at the cabin that Amanda and he stayed at."

Betty responded quickly as if playing a guessing game.

"That's got to be Samantha's cabin. I know where it is."

"Mrs. Rogers can you come with us to talk to Stefan, he is going to be upset that he was lied to. You understand why we did what we did...don't you?" Betty said in a shaking voice. She had tears in her eyes, she was heartbroken that they had been lying to the Rogers but she did what she thought was best for her autistic son.

Jim told the group that there was a cold front pushing through, there was a strong chance of heavy rain.
Stefan's mom turned to Betty.
"Betty I am the one that is sorry, let's go get Stefan. He loves

Amanda so much... he would die for that girl."

The women hugged. Jim shook Bob's hand and told him that
they would go straight to the hospital from Eagle's Nest. Betty
told Stefan's mom that she could stay at the hotel with them;
there was plenty of room. Mrs. Rogers packed her bags, and
they all got on board the helicopter. Stefan's father stayed
home; after Vietnam he was not able to ride in a helicopter
without serious flashbacks. After all, they were just going to
take Stefan to visit Amanda.

This was not the way the parents wanted to meet. One child
on the edge of life and the other child dying inside. The flight
to Eagle's Nest was about 2 hours from Stefan's Parents house.
When the helicopter touched down in the field in front of the
cabin Melissa came out see who it was. As Mrs. Rogers and
Betty walked towards the door, Melissa knew who they were.
They looked like their children. Betty was an older Amanda.
Mrs. Rogers had Stefan's nose and eyes.

"Melissa?" Stefan's mom asked.

"I am Mrs. Rogers and this is Betty, Amanda's Mom. Where is
Stefan we need to talk to him?"
Melissa broke done and started crying.

"I could not stop him; he has gone to Eagle's nest."
It started to rain...

"Can we go inside? Tell us what is going on."

"Melissa, Amanda is alive."
Melissa put her hand over her mouth and starting crying again.
"What do you mean you could not stop him?"

Melissa could not speak, she handed Stefan's mom the note.

"We have to tell him! The park is closed. It will take too long to reach the rangers to open it. I know where the key is and a short cut to the rock face."

Stefan's mom read the note as tears fell to the ground. She looked up at Melissa and asked, "Did you know he was going to do this, is that why you called me this morning?"

Melissa could not speak she just nodded her head up and down. "I – I tried to talk him out of it, that is why I am here. He would not allow me to go with him... We need to go; he was waiting for the rain... It's raining we have to go!"

The women got into the helicopter and headed to Eagle's Nest. They landed in a field across from the secret gate. The rain was now coming down harder. Melissa was scared that Stefan would not be there that they were too late. They all ran through the woods towards the rock face. The only saving grace was that it had just started to rain. As they got closer

Melissa started calling out Stefan's name.

"Stefan...Stefan..."

Melissa was faster than the mothers – they were several yards behind her. Stefan was standing on the edge of the face looking down.

"I told you not to come... Why did you come?"

"Stefan please don't be mad, please don't do this, Stefan, Amanda..."   Before she could finish her sentence Stefan started yelling at her.

"All I asked was for you tell my story, I do not need saving... I loved her, why can't you accept that I don't want to live without her."

"She is alive Stefan...Amanda is alive!"

"What are you saying...? I don't believe you, Stop! You are lying.

Don't come any closer!"

"No—please—no..."

Stefan turned to step off

"BABY NO! Amanda is ALIVE!"

Stefan recognized the voice... it was not Melissa!

"Mom, what are you doing here?"
"She is Alive..."

"You are lying, Melissa told you to lie to me. You told her…
Didn't you!
Melissa you promised you wouldn't tell… you promised!"

The rain was coming down harder though they were only a few feet apart it was beginning to get dark.

"I trusted you Melissa!"

"Stefan she is alive!"
"Listen to your mom."

"I don't believe you; Mom leave… please Mom, leave."

Then Stefan saw Amanda's mom walking towards him, he thought it was Amanda.

"Amanda! Amanda My God it is you! Amanda…" He ran towards her, but as he got closer he could tell it was not her.
"Stefan I am her mom, you have to believe me she is alive and needs you."

Melissa was crying, shaking not from the cold but the fear that Stefan felt betrayed. She knew that his project was at stake.

"Stefan she needs you... You still can save her."

"Honey she is at Saint Anthony's Hospital; we told the media she died because of Michael... she is in bad shape Stefan; you are the only one that can save her. Her heart beats faster every time we say your name...she loves you Stefan, she is alive."

Stefan was confused and scared; he knew that if he went with them and they were lying then he would not complete the project. His mom had never lied to him, but this was about suicide. It does not count as a lie.

"Melissa, is she really alive?"

"Yes... Stefan, the pilot is the one that found her. She loves you Stefan please don't do this... I was willing to let you go through with this because I knew you loved her... She is alive and she needs you. Let her hear you voice Stefan, please... she needs you."

Stefan turned and walked towards the edge of the cliff. His mother took a deep breath as she watched her son step to the edge of life and death.

"No Stefan, please no... I love you!"
"I love you Stefan! Stefan, she is alive, damn it! Listen to me, please."

Stefan turned around and looked at Melissa.

"Amanda loves you—don't do this. She needs you Stefan."

He looked at the sculpture, the last kiss. He looked at his mom and Amanda's mom. He looked at Melissa: a woman that was willing to give up everything to make sure he finished his project.

"It is a change order... You are still going to be with her." Melissa said hoping that he would realize she was telling the truth.

Stefan looked back into the darkness.

"Stefan's mom spoke up...
"Stefan I am your mother; I brought you into this world. If Amanda is not alive I will bring you back here. Baby she is alive, she needs you, and we understand you are willing to die for her. Melissa did not tell us what is going on; you left me a note. She never lied to you, she still is not lying to you."

"Please Stefan! Amanda is alive, and she needs you." Melissa cried out as if it was her last chance to convince him.

Julie stepped out from the darkness, she was wearing her Saint Anthony's shirt. "Stefan I am Amanda's nurse... you have to believe us, she needs you."

Melissa had her hand against her lips trembling; everyone had tears in their eyes.

Amanda's mom spoke up,
"Stefan you know about Michael... Stefan, Amanda is in bad shape, she needs you to come back. Please for Michael's sake, come with us."

Stefan knew that Amanda would die for Michael; he meant the world to her. Stefan looked into the darkness, with toes over the edge and the rock slippery, it came down to trust. What did his heart tell him? The rain began to come down even harder. Stefan could not see the women any more they were blurred forms moving in the rain. Stefan was confused, his sense of direction was distorted. He thought he was moving away from the edge but actually stepped into the darkness. Melissa screamed and reached out for him. Stefan's mom cried out his name – as his body lost balance he reached out. He could not see the face of Melissa but his hand grabbed hers. There was nothing the mothers could do, they were too far away. It was now up to God and love to save him. Stefan weighed much more than Melissa, his body was too far into the darkness to make it back alone. Melissa started sliding towards the edge. She loved him, though she promised to let him go, this was different...Amanda was alive! Melissa held onto him. They both were on the edge of life, two people that were deeply in love fighting to stay alive. Stefan heard her crying, screaming his name.

"Hold on Stefan, hold on!"

Then it happened in a flash just as Amanda had fallen, Stefan felt the separation from the ground.
  His mother was crying out to God.
"God please, NO!"
Then Like God himself reaching down to earth Stefan was grabbed by Jim, the pilot for SkyVac. Betty grabbed Melissa and pulled her back away from the edge as Jim fought to save Stefan's life. Jim had reached Stefan just as he was slipping off. Jim was ex-special forces, with arms of steel and a heart to match. He was not going to let Amanda down. Once on stable ground Stefan hugged Melissa, she was crying... She held the sides of his face.

"She is alive Stefan, she is alive."
They hugged each other and cried.

"Stefan we need to get going the storm is getting worse, we need to get back to the helicopter."
Jim said as he pointed in the direction of the trail.
Amanda's mom hugged Melissa,
"Thank you. God Bless you."

They made their way through the woods to the helicopter.

As they approached Saint Anthony, Julie heard Jim on the radio.

"Saint Anthony, this is SkyVac 1, do you copy?"

"SkyVac 1, this is Saint Anthony, we read you... Go ahead."

"Saint Anthony, this is SkyVac 1, we are inbound with Stefan Rogers, and we are requesting permission to land, ETA 10 minutes... over."

"SkyVac 1, you are clear for South platform."

Julie reached over and squeezed Amanda's mom's hand. "She is going to be alright."